WYATT

OVERWATCH DIVISION

COCO MILLER

COCO MILLER ROMANCE

Want to be notified when I release my next book or give away freebies?

JOIN MY LIST

Coco On Facebook

Coco On Instagram

www.CocoMillerRomance.com

LICENSE NOTE

BOOKS BY COCO

Big City Billionaires
Faking For Mr. Pope
Virgin Escort For Mr. Vaughn
Pretending for Mr. Parker

Red Bratva Billionaires
MAXIM
SERGEI
VIKTOR

The Overwatch Division
WYATT
ASA
CESAR

INTRODUCTION

He's an ex-military man working through his demons. She's a high-powered lawyer looking to shake things up. Sometimes the very answer you've been searching for can be found right where you started...

Kendra lives a high-powered life in New York City but something is missing. She visits home to shake things up and that's when she notices her brother's best friend, Wyatt. The hot man in front of her is nothing like she remembered at all.

Wyatt is back from Afghanistan and whoring his

way through woman after woman in an attempt to forget his time overseas. One look at Kendra though, and he falls hard and fast for the out-of-town beauty.

Will this unlikely couple even stand a chance at a happily ever after? Especially once Wyatt's best friend, who is also Kendra's brother, finds out what they've been up to?

WYATT is a sweet and steamy, stand-alone, military romance. It is not appropriate for readers under 18 due to sizzling HAWT love scenes!

CHAPTER ONE

KENDRA

"I'LL HAVE ANOTHER COSMO," I say pushing my glass to Gail, the head bartender at *Gail's Bar*. I don't know her, but there are plenty of people in this bar that do, so I've heard her name several times.

Gail's is the only bar within a fifteen-mile radius in this area, and I heard it's home to a great selection of beers. Mixed cocktails, however, aren't their strong suit. There's not enough cranberry juice in it. It tastes like pure alcohol. But at least I'll get drunk faster and for a lot less money than it takes in New York.

"You got it. Are you sure you don't want something to eat?" she asks while making my drink.

"No thanks, just the drink," I mumble twisting a napkin in my hand.

When she places the drink in front of me, I pay her and take a sip. I look around the bar and figure there must not be many out-of-towners here because they all seem to know each other. There are many people here and I assume that's because it's a Friday night.

I'll admit, I'm enjoying the people watching. It's probably the most fun I've had in a long time. That pretty much describes how boring my life has become.

Needing an escape, maybe looking for a bit of excitement, has brought me back upstate and to the Day's Ranch. I spent all of my summers here as a kid.

My parents ended up buying the ranch after my brother and I graduated high school. Then they moved here permanently. Now my brother works for them at the resort.

I wasn't willing to leave the city. I had dreams to accomplish and goals to reach which I've been lucky enough to do. However, now I feel like I need more, something different. So when I could no longer take the repetitiveness of everyday life, something told me this is where I needed to be. So here I am.

Hearing a deep voice in the distance draws my attention. I look around until my eyes land on what has to be the sexiest guy I've ever seen. Dark hair, muscles that look clearly defined beneath his t-shirt, and I can tell he is popular with the women because they are circling around him, waiting for their chance. Like buzzards.

I look back toward Gail and smile. "Who's Mr. Popular?"

She laughs as she wipes down the bar. "That is the town heartthrob."

"The women are practically salivating over him. It's a wonder all that attention doesn't go to his head."

"Oh, trust me it has. He has slept with almost every tourist of legal age and a vagina. He knows he is the hottest thing walking on the planet and he takes full advantage of it."

"That's unfortunate. There's something so sad about man whores. Like they're starving for something mommy didn't give them."

"Well, he may have a slight excuse. He came back from serving overseas really fucked up in the head. Whatever happened over there did a number on him. He lives recklessly. Wyatt Drake just doesn't give a shit about much except getting drunk and getting laid."

Wait ... did you say Wyatt Drake? No way. It can't be the same Wyatt Drake that I grew up with. The same scrawny kid that used to collect baseball cards, ride his bike up and down past my house, and tell me the most ridiculous stories. Because that Wyatt was my brother's best friend, and he sure as hell didn't look anything like this Wyatt.

I glance back at him just to make sure when Gail places her hand on mine.

"Don't bother with him, sweetie. He's basically just a pretty face. He sleeps with all the visitors we get, not only here at the bar but also at Day's Ranch where he stays. He'll just use you and move on. He hasn't been the same since he returned from active duty."

Active duty? I didn't know Wyatt entered the service. And he'll just use me, huh? Maybe this is exactly what I need. I mean the reason I drove down here from New York City was to break out of my rat race. A one-night stand could be a huge start. The fact that he's not a total stranger is great, and the idea that he hangs out at the ranch where I am staying, well that is just a bonus.

"You should listen to the lady. Wyatt's a great guy, but I sure as hell wouldn't trust him around any woman I know," says a guy who has just plopped down next to me.

"Thanks, I appreciate the advice..." I let the last word drag out giving him the opportunity to introduce himself.

"Leon," he says, tossing back his beer.

"Well thanks, Leon. I'm Kendra," I say, but he doesn't pay much attention. He is talking to Gail, so I decide to just take Wyatt in.

He looks like a bad boy, which is such a difference from the Wyatt I knew, and a huge turn-on for me. All the guys I've been with are exactly like my life, boring. Especially the last guy I was with, Kevin.

He had no sense of humor, didn't enjoy going out because he'd be too tired in the morning, even on a Friday night.

Worst of all, he was the worst sex I'd ever had. He didn't like to fool around; he just went right for it, and it lasted—on a good day—five minutes. Checking out Wyatt, I can tell he'd be amazing in bed. Just the way his body moves is sexy as hell.

I think back to when I left the city the other night. I was sitting in my office going over the paperwork I needed for a case I was working on and I couldn't concentrate on it. The last few weeks had been like that. I used to live for work. I thrived on being in the courtroom, working long nights and not having a life at all. But something was changing, and I knew I needed to get away to figure it out.

Walking into my boss's office, I told him I needed time off and considering I hadn't taken a sick day or vacation day in years; I had time on my side.

Pulling out of my thoughts, I order yet another drink before looking back to my new favorite view. I watch him laughing with a few of his friends or who I think are his friends, and it reminds me of how long it's been since I laughed like that. I can't even remember what it's like to laugh and actually mean it. To find something so funny that it just comes pouring out of you.

I take a deep breath and toss back the rest of my drink, trying to numb the pain I'm feeling. I have no idea what I've been doing with my life. Yes, I make great money, live in an upscale loft, and own more clothes than I'll ever wear. But what's the point?

I have no one to share it with, no one who can make me laugh, and no one who can make life exciting.

That's what this vacation is all about, and I think Wyatt may be the key or at least a quick fix.

CHAPTER TWO

WYATT

ANOTHER FRIDAY NIGHT of hanging out at Gail's. I don't see any visitors, so I'm just relaxing after a long week of busting my ass at work. I'll admit, I would love to find a beautiful woman to take home for the night, but tomorrow is another day.

A lot of the regulars are here and, as usual, flirting with me, but it's something I've gotten used to. They all know I sleep around, and that I will not settle down, so they all want to be the one who changes me.

I wouldn't be surprised if they bet on it, but I don't care. I know what I want and it sure as hell isn't a relationship. I love women, but I don't trust them. So I guess you could say, I use them. I'm not proud of it; it's just how I am.

I'm about to get up to grab a beer when I notice this beautiful woman sitting at the bar. She catches my eye. She is definitely not from around here. I can tell by the sexy yet classy dress she's wearing, the way she seems to sit with almost an arrogance about her, and that crazy-looking drink in her hand. Regulars don't drink fruity shit.

Maybe my night is looking up after all.

She's gorgeous and totally different from the townies around here with her reddish-brown skin and her sleek black hair. I keep watching her, trying to figure her out. It's a little game I like to play before I make my move.

She is probably passing through because as lucky as I am with women, they rarely look as stunning as her. The women who vacation here are pretty and sexy, but this woman is on another level. Maybe she's married or engaged; no that can't be right because the guy would be a fool to leave her alone at a bar. Damn, she's a hard one to figure out.

Most of the time, I can guess if they are

running away for the weekend, partying with friends, or vacationing with family. I've lived here long enough to study them all. I'd just finished high school when mommy dearest decided to walk out on me and my pop's, we moved to Day's Ranch.

I remember wanting to stay at my home in the city, but I couldn't let my pop handle moving alone. When I found out it was the resort my best friend, Malik's, parents had bought, it was an easier decision.

Shaking my head to clear those unnecessary thoughts, I notice the visiting beauty is checking me out and I figure it's time to make my move. I smirk as I make my way over to her.

She keeps her clear, deep brown eyes on me the entire time, watching every move I make very carefully. When I reach her I rest against the bar and she turns to face me with a slight look of curiosity across her face.

"There was no way I could not find out the name of the most beautiful woman I've ever seen," I say pouring on the charm.

A small smile tugs at her lips and she says, "Kendra."

"Kendra, that's a great name. I'm Wyatt. Wyatt Drake."

A look I can't quite describe crosses her face.

I extend my hand and she places her delicate one in mine. "What brings you here, Kendra?"

"A little me time," she says with a blush making its way to her face.

"Me time is always good. So where are you heading?" I ask as I signal to Gail for another beer.

"I'm headed right here. I'm staying at Day's Ranch."

I can't stop the smile that breaks out. She's staying at the resort, how convenient. This just got a whole lot easier.

"No kidding. That's where I'm from," I say, moving a little closer to her.

She's definitely liking the attention I'm showing her, that much is clear. I also seem to make her nervous, which is a major turn-on. I reach out my hand and rest it on her knee.

"How long are you staying?"

"I'm not sure yet. Only time will tell," she says as she tosses back the rest of her drink.

Damn, she's beautiful.

"Kendra, come dance with me," I say, removing my hand from her knee and holding it for her to take. Without hesitation, she grabs my hand and I lead her out to the little dance floor. There is no band here tonight, but the music is still flowing. I pull her close to me and we slowly move to the beat.

"Where are you from?"

"New York City."

I run my hands lightly up and down her back and she searches my eyes, looking for something but I do not understand what.

"No kidding. I grew up in New York," I say.

She suddenly stops dancing and pulls away.

"I wasn't sure at first but are you Wyatt Drake, from Long Island? Was your best friend, Malik Collins?"

Well damn, how the hell could she know that.

I tilt my head, lifting an eyebrow. "Yeah, that's me. Who the hell are you?"

Laughing to herself, she bites her lip. "Wyatt, it's me, Kendra Collins."

"No fucking way."

My best friend's baby sister has grown the hell up. See this is the problem with Malik's paranoid ass not using social media. I almost felt up his damn sister without even knowing it. I haven't seen her since she was a kid.

"Way," she chuckles.

The next hour consists of us dancing and her

drinking more of those colorful drinks of hers. If she keeps this up, I'm going to need to call her an Uber or drive her to the resort myself.

We get a bit more handsy with each other, which is making this situation that much harder. It's making everything harder.

"Kendra, does Malik even know you're here?" I ask while she waits for her next drink.

"No, no one does yet. I just up and left. I needed to do something to make my life less boring. I'm tired of it. I want excitement. I want sex. I want someone who will make me laugh and make life worthwhile."

She's drunk... no, she's trashed. Her pupils are huge, her eyes are glassy, and she's slurring her words. What's more, is she's an honest drunk. She's looking for someone to make her life less boring? That sounds like a job right up my alley.

Everything she just mentioned is what I want, until she mentions making her life worthwhile. That I avoid. Even though I'd love to have her in my bed, there's no way I am getting involved. Too many red flags. Too complicated.

"I'm lonely, Wyatt. I just need to figure out what I've been doing wrong with my life. I want to have fun. I know you like to have fun," she slurs.

Something about the way she is talking and the crazy amount of alcohol she's had doesn't add up. I don't normally care, but this is Kendra Collins. She's not just any regular girl. No she's so much more than that.

CHAPTER THREE

KENDRA

WAKING UP, I crack my eyes open and am assaulted by the light. I groan and grab my head, immediately regretting the amount of alcohol I consumed last night.

I never drink like that and the way I'm feeling right now, I'll never do it again. My head is pounding, my stomach is turning, I'm sweating, and my hair is all over my damn head.

It's official, I feel like shit.

I sit up slowly and notice I am just wearing a t-shirt. The thing is, it's not my t-shirt. It's huge on me and smells like cologne. The realization hits me, and I cover my mouth with my hand. "Oh my God," I whisper to myself. My head really starts pounding, and I decide I need to take something before I even think about anything else.

I climb out of bed and open the door from my small bedroom. I step into the living room and scream out when I see Wyatt standing in the kitchen, shirtless. My head is punishing me and starts throbbing as I say, "What the hell are you doing here?" As if I didn't already know.

"Well, look who finally woke up," he says, walking over to me and handing me three ibuprofen and a bottle of water. "Take this and after you shower, we can go grab some breakfast to soak up the rest of the alcohol. I'm sure is still swimming in your body."

What the fuck?

Who the hell does he think he is? He's just going to dismiss what happened last night and take me out to breakfast. What for? A thank you for the lay?

I know that last night I thought a one-night stand with my brother's best friend would be a good idea, but that was before it actually happened. I mean it's Wyatt. How did I let this happen?

I quickly swallow down the pills and wrap my arms around myself. "What the hell happened last night? Well, I mean obviously I know what happened, but why would you even want to have sex with a woman that drunk?"

He chuckles and shakes his head. "Nothing happened last night."

"You expect me to believe that? I'm wearing your t-shirt and I wake up with you in my room, but nothing happened? You know what, I don't even want to hear the details of it." How stupid does he think I am?

"Hey, I said nothing happened," he says, crossing his arms over his muscular chest in a defensive way.

"Right, I'm sure that's why you're still here," I say before turning to walk to the bathroom.

He grabs my arm and spins me around to look at him. He looks pissed, but I don't give a shit. He's the one standing in my cabin shirtless, with his incredible upper body on display. It's so obvious what happened, and he refuses to admit it. He moves his face a little closer to mine and says, "Nothing happened. That's not the kind of guy I am."

I laugh and pull my arm out of his hold.

"Actually, that is exactly the kind of guy you are. Now if you'll excuse me, I need to shower. When I get out, I'd like for you to be long gone, Wyatt Drake."

"You want me to tell you what happened last night?" he growls, looking at me with daggers in his eyes.

"Wyatt, look I already told you I don't want details. Please get out of my cabin," I say, walking into the bathroom and closing the door.

I don't know who the hell he thinks he is. What kind of guy sleeps with a woman who is clearly too drunk to give any sort of true consent, not to mention he's Malik's best friend. Then act like nothing happened the next day while standing in my kitchen shirtless. You need not be a fucking genius to figure it out. You do, however, need to be a complete asshole to lie about it.

LATER IN THE DAY, after a long visit with my mom, who said my dad and Malik won't be back for another two weeks from a hunting trip they went on, I decide to take a trip into town to get some groceries. There is no food at my place. I have no idea how long I'm going to stay, but I need food. When I get to the small store, I get a shopping cart then make my way through the aisles grabbing a few things I need — completely bypassing the aisle of alcohol.

I can't stop thinking about Wyatt, and not because of his sexy body that was right there in my face earlier but because he was even more of an asshole than I thought. When Gail told me to stay away from him, I should have listened. I figured he was Wyatt. And maybe, just a guy who likes to sleep around, and I guess part of that is right. I just didn't think he was the kind of guy to lie about it the next day. What's the point of that?

I don't know what it is about the men that come crashing into my life, but all of them suck. None of them are like Wyatt, but the complete opposite, boring and predictable. I knew I needed a change, but Wyatt Drake is not the change I need. He was a mistake.

Thinking about how pissed I am with myself as well as Wyatt, I'm not paying much attention to what I'm doing when I accidentally hit another shopping cart.

"Oh shit. I'm so sorry. I'm not paying any attention. Are you all right?" A good looking guy smiles at me, and for the first time since I woke up, I feel a smile pulling at my lips.

"I'm fine," he says, checking me out, and I'll admit it feels pretty good to have his attention. "It's my fault, I have my cart just sitting here. I just can't figure out what kind of cheese is best for this wine I just picked up."

I lean over and hand him a mild cheddar. "Here, you can't go wrong with this one."

He takes it from me and drops it in the cart. "Thank you so much. I'm sure my wife will be happy with this."

Are you fucking kidding me? I just smile and say, "I'm sure she will. I'm sorry again."

I walk away and roll my eyes. I think right now it's best to just spend a little time with myself. I'm obviously not good at picking men. Some are boring, some are married, and some are complete lying assholes.

CHAPTER FOUR

WYATT

I'M SITTING on my deck looking out into the lush forest that surrounds me. Taking another long sip of my beer, I shake my head to clear it of thoughts of Kendra. She was a complete bitch this morning and didn't even want to hear an explanation as to what I was doing there. She just assumed something happened.

I don't know why she thinks she knows me, but obviously, she doesn't. I haven't seen her since I was a kid just out of high school. She doesn't know the man I've become. She doesn't know shit about me. As pissed as I may be though, she still consumes my thoughts.

I'd never take advantage of a woman.

I might sleep around, but I've never been with a woman who didn't consent to being with me. I never have nor will I ever sleep with a woman so drunk that she can hardly stand. It bothers me she thinks so little of me, and I can't understand why. Why do I care?

Normally, I couldn't care less what someone thinks of me, but with her it's different. I want her to understand that I was there taking care of her, not taking advantage of her.

I want her to know the real me, not the Wyatt that I let everyone see. I want to explain. I want her to listen. I want her respect. I realize that she is Malik's baby sister, and I should back off, but damn it, I'm drawn to her.

I throw back the rest of my beer, just as my buddy Todd drops by. "Hey man, what's up?" I ask.

"Wyatt, we need to go to the bar tonight. I heard there's going to be an awesome band playing after open mic night, and when the bands are there so are the chicks," he says with an excited grin.

My first reaction is to say no. The last thing on

my mind is spending the night out trolling for barflies after what happened (or what didn't happen) with Kendra, but maybe it's just what I need. Maybe I need to just jump right back in the saddle on my horse again and get my mind off of my friend's baby sister. I'm giving what happened with her way too much air time.

"All right, let me just change my shirt and we can go. I'll drive."

When we get to Gail's Bar, I'm not surprised to see the number of people here since it's open mic night. Todd and I walk up to the bar and Gail hands us each a beer.

"Boys," she addresses us with a grin.

"Gail."

We accept our drinks and take a seat.

"Hey Wyatt, how did things go with the beautiful bombshell you picked up last night?" Gail asks.

"Yeah, did you tap that?" Todd asks as well.

My body shifts uncomfortably at the mention of last night.

"I took her home and made sure she was good. Not a very exciting night," I say nonchalantly as I draw back a sip of my beer.

"Sure, that's what happened," Gail mocks, but

before I make my defense known she is off helping another customer. I shake my head and look over at Todd.

He grins and slaps my back. "I'm sure you made sure she was *all* good."

"Todd, nothing happened."

"Nothing happened that you want to talk about because let's be real, when has nothing ever happened with you?"

"Todd–"

"Naw, I get it, man. You can just tell me about the next woman," he says chuckling as he walks off to a table closer to the stage so we can sit and watch the performances.

I'm regretting coming out already. Gail I could give a shit about, but Todd doesn't even believe me and that pisses me off. I've never lied to him. He knows as much about me as Malik does. Why he thinks I'd lie on my dick is beyond me, but honestly, I couldn't give a shit right now.

I follow Todd over to the table just as Jim and Dave take a seat. The four of us and Malik grew up together and through the years, we've been through a lot together.

We've always got each other's backs, even in the case of those deceitful women who forget to mention their boyfriends... or in Dave's case, husband. When I left for the military, these men stood by me. And when I returned they had my back yet again.

Thinking about Todd's reaction again makes me realize it's no wonder no one believes that I didn't sleep with Kendra. When I leave the bar with a woman, I always sleep with her.

A lot of the visitors at Day's Ranch have definitely visited my bed, and I'm not ashamed of that fact. I enjoy women and they enjoy me. It's always mutual, always respectful. There's nothing wrong with that.

"Hey Wyatt, how was last night? I saw you leave with that chick, who is fucking hot by the way," Jim asks as the first guy climbs on stage for open mic.

"Actually, nothing happened," I repeat myself.

"Yeah, right. If you didn't get a piece of that beautiful ass last night then you're slipping."

All three of them chuckle loudly, and I shake my head. I'm getting pissed off at this point, and am ready to tell them just who she is. They shouldn't be talking about Malik's sister like this. Even though her ass is spectacular.

"Yo, I'm fucking serious. I didn't sleep with

her. Why the hell is that so hard for you to understand? Do you have any idea who she is?"

I've lost their attention and turn to see what they are looking at. Two beautiful women who just walked in. They are with an older man and a dude that looks to be about their age. I've never seen them around, so I'm sure they are here for open mic night.

"Damn, look at that one chick with the red hair. She's hot and looks like she could use a little company tonight," Dave says, never looking away from her.

"Make sure she isn't married to that older guy before you make a move," I say, causing them all to chuckle again.

Gail interrupts our laughter when she announces that Alex is about to take the stage. We sit back and listen to him and damn, he's got a great voice. It always amazes me when people as talented as he comes into this bar for open mic. He should be singing on a stage in front of thousands of people, not just a few handfuls worth.

I won't be surprised if one day I turn on the radio and hear his voice, though. He's that good, plus he's singing a song he wrote. The guy is multi-talented.

After a few more people get up and sing — no one nearly as talented as Alex — I go to the bathroom. Before I even make my way to it, I'm stopped by no less than five of the bar's regulars telling me they saw me leave with Kendra last night. It's making my blood boil at this point, and I have no one to blame but myself.

This is the reputation I've made. I sleep around and never get involved. No one views me any other way, and for the first time ever, I don't like it.

When I get back to the table, I sit down and look around at the guys. I can't do it. Being here just pisses me off more. I need to get out of here and confront Kendra. I want to make her understand that nothing happened because even if no one else believes me; I want her to.

"Guys, I need to call it a night. I have something I need to take care of. I'll see you at work tomorrow." I don't even give them time to question me; I just get up and leave.

The drive over to Kendra's place just pisses me off more. I don't know if I'm angrier with myself or everyone else. I still don't understand why I give a fuck all of a sudden.

That's not true.

I know it's because of who she is and my quest

to have her respect. I don't want her thinking I'm some bar bum who gets wasted and sleeps with every random woman who is attracted to me.

I get out of my crappy Toyota pickup and slam the door. Knocking on the door, I can hear her moving around inside. She pushes open the door and looks at me with disgust.

"We need to talk," I say, leaning against the railing.

"No, actually we don't," she says and goes to close the door in my face.

I wedge my foot inside of the doorway. "Is this how you treat a veteran?"

I try this route and it only pisses her off more. So, I grab the door to keep her from closing it and move closer.

"Believe me, Kendra, you'd know if we slept together. That I guarantee," I say in my most seductive voice with a smirk on my face. "You'd feel it. You'd know."

She pushes me away from her and stands in the doorway with her arms crossed, with that same look of disgust on her face.

"You are the cockiest son of a bitch I've ever met. You had to come over here this late, just to say if we slept together I'd remember? Well, you know what, Wyatt, maybe it's something I don't want to remember. Maybe it was just that unmemorable."

"I didn't come over here to be a cocky bastard. I came over here to try to make you understand that nothing happened with us. I came over here to assure you that I don't sleep with inebriated women." She rolls her eyes but I keep going. "You don't even know me, yet you assume you do. We haven't seen each other since we were kids," I say in a much calmer voice than the attitude she is throwing at me.

"You're right. I don't know you, not since you left. However, I clearly know your type. The whole bar knows your type. You sleep around, never giving a shit about anyone else but yourself.

"Sometimes you don't even bother to get to know more than her name. Am I getting warm?" she says in an angry whisper. She's right, though. She is a hundred percent right.

I softly laugh but out of disappointment and say, "You're right."

She gets a cocky smile on her face and I turn to walk away. When I reach my truck, I turn to look at her. "That night, though, I did the right thing. I took care of you, which is a lot more than the average dude in that bar would have done."

I get into the truck and slam my door.

And then I try to forget about the beautiful ass that slams the cabin door in response.

CHAPTER FIVE

KENDRA

AFTER WYATT LEAVES, I go into the house and sit down on the couch. No longer am I interested in TV or this bowl of ice cream. I'm so confused.

What kind of guy comes to your place to tell you nothing happened and then admits that he normally sleeps around? I felt satisfied when he admitted to his hoe-ish ways, but when he said that he actually did the right thing and took care of me, I don't know; I think I believe him.

The way he said it with such sadness in his voice, it felt truthful. He never broke eye contact with me; he didn't sweat or smile. Holy shit, what kind of lawyer am I?

I should be able to know immediately if someone is lying and now I'm questioning it all. I think I may have judged him on what I heard at the bar that night. I don't know him, not anymore, yet I assumed I knew it all. I was a bitch.

I go into the bedroom and pull out Wyatt's shirt that I washed earlier and frown. When I told him to leave yesterday, I didn't bother taking it off, and he didn't ask for it. Maybe I shouldn't have been such a bitch and rushed to label him. I should have listened to what he had to say instead of kicking him out of my trailer.

Oh my God, what kind of person am I? I mean he is one of my brother's best friends. I should have given him the benefit of the doubt.

I flop down on the bed and cover my face. Even though no one can see me, I feel the need to hide. I'm humiliated that I was so awful to him, not once but twice. I'm sure he thinks I'm a bitch and he wouldn't be wrong considering how I treated him the other day.

Not wanting to think about it anymore, I close my eyes and hope that sleep pulls me under quickly.

CHAPTER SIX

KENDRA

AFTER A RESTLESS NIGHT OF SLEEP, I get up and shower. It's strange not to have a schedule. I'm used to getting up, showering, going to work, and repeating the whole routine again every day.

Having this time to myself is wonderful yet confusing. I feel like I should do something, not just sit around drinking coffee. I look around the beautiful resort my parents have put their blood, sweat, and tears into, and decide that today I will go exploring. It's been a long time since I've been here and I'd like to reacquaint myself.

Changing into a pair of cut-off jean shorts and

a pink tank top, I toss on my flip-flops and head out. Following the different trails, I admire the surrounding beauty. There is such a vast variety of trees, bushes, and flowers all mixed throughout the resort that I could walk around for weeks and never identify them all.

One path leads me to the lake, and I love the tranquil feel when I reach the water's edge. I sit down and take it all in. It is so quiet and peaceful. The only sounds I hear are birds chirping, leaves rustling, and the water kissing the shoreline. It relaxes me, pulling me into a meditative state.

In the city, I never take the time to enjoy the world around me. It moves at a sprinter's pace and you do your best to keep up. There is no time to slow down and enjoy yourself, not if you're trying to climb the corporate ladder.

The sounds I usually hear are honking horns, construction, and loud talking, and that's just on the way to work. Once I'm there, it is the sound of my keyboard, the phone ringing, and the sound of the damn clock hand ticking, taunting me with how much time is passing while I do nothing to make me truly happy.

I bring my focus back to my stunning

surroundings. I'm sitting a bit secluded, letting the sun beat down on me.

I look across the way when I hear hammering and notice a group of guys working on a cabin. I don't know how I missed it; I guess I was focusing too much on the scenery around me. Although now that they have gained my attention, I am pulled in to watching them. They are joking with each other and look like they are having a great time working. It makes me a little jealous that I don't feel that same enjoyment in my job.

They turn some music on, and while I can't make out the song, the beat carries over to me and I nod my head to the rhythm. One guy yells to another trying to get his attention over the music before he laughs at something inside that I can't see. I look over and son of a bitch; it's Wyatt.

He's shirtless, showing off that incredible upper body of his. Regret that I had pushed aside resurfaces. I don't know where I get the courage, but I'm on my feet and walking over to the cabin. The need to apologize to him is overwhelming.

The closer I get the louder everything is—the hammering, the shouting, the music, and the laughter. Before I'm even to the cabin, one of the guys notices me and flashes me a flirty grin. I smile back and walk over to him, thinking he seems to be friendly.

"Hi. Is it possible for me to talk to Wyatt real fast? I won't take up much of his time."

"Whatever he did to you, I'll fix it," he says giving me a wink and I laugh.

"Kendra? What are you doing?" Wyatt says from behind me, shock clear in his voice.

I turn around and take a deep breath. I try to compose myself because seeing him shirtless is screwing with my head. I have no idea how he will react to me walking up on him while he is at work.

"Can I just talk to you for a minute, please?"

He nods his head and hands his hammer to the guy I was talking to. "Jim, I'll be right back."

I follow him away from all the noise, taking notice of his muscular back as his walks. I shake my head, trying to focus on my apology. He stops and turns around, crossing his arms over his bare chest.

"You forget to throw in a dig last night?" he says with a mix of hurt and anger in his voice.

"Wyatt, I'm so sorry. I never should have rushed to judge you. I don't have any memory of what happened the other night, and I should have believed you," I say in my best attorney voice. "That was wrong of me."

"You know what it doesn't matter. I need to get back to work." He goes to push past me, and I stop him with my hands on his chest. His tight wall of muscles almost renders me speechless.

"I fucked up, all right? I admit it. Everything I did was the complete opposite of what I was taught. You should have been innocent until proven guilty, but I had you guilty without even hearing your case."

He doesn't say a word, so I continue. "I wanted a night of fun; that's what I set out for. I saw you in the bar, and I'll be honest, I was attracted to you. Then Gail told me your name, and it shocked me. So when you came over, I was so overwhelmed with figuring out if it was the Wyatt I knew, I kept drinking."

I shake my head and look out at the lake. "I don't know what else to say. I know you think I'm a bitch and I don't blame you, I've been one. I'm sorry for everything."

He says nothing, but he doesn't leave either. I don't know what I should do at this point. I'll admit it, I'm attracted to him. I want to make this right.

"I think maybe it was my guilt talking yesterday. I drank too much, I couldn't remember shit, and the next day I just wanted to believe so badly that someone as sexy as you would be attracted to someone like me, so I hoped we did something." I admit, shocking even myself.

He closes his eyes for a second before snapping them back open just as quickly. "Kendra, I did right by you that night, but don't let it fool you. I came over to you at the bar for something else entirely. I didn't know you were Malik's sister. I just saw a beautiful woman at the bar."

My pulse races as I wonder what things he would have done to me if I hadn't drunk so much. I smile and look back to the cabin he's working at.

"So, I guess I shouldn't keep you. But do you think you'd like to come over for dinner tonight?"

He gives me a sexy grin and asks, "Are you asking me on a date, Kendra?"

I laugh, mostly out of embarrassment and shake my head. "No. I thought it would be nice to get to know my brother's friend, without alcohol."

"I get off work at five," is all he says and walks past me to go back to work. I guess that means he'll be over. For the first time in as long as I can remember, I have butterflies swarming inside of my stomach.

Wow, this is new.

CHAPTER SEVEN

WYATT

WHEN I GET off of work, I go home and take a shower. Since Kendra left the job site earlier today, I haven't been able to think about anything else. To say it shocked me to see her there is an understatement. I could tell she's a woman who isn't used to giving an apology, and so I let her off easy. I wouldn't say I've gained her respect, but then again I wouldn't say she has mine.

Once I get myself showered and dressed in a black t-shirt and khaki shorts, I go outside and climb into my golf cart. I'm not expecting anything from tonight. I don't even know if going to her place is a good idea. Hell, getting involved with her in any form isn't a good idea. She doesn't need someone like me in her life, not to mention Malik will beat my ass, but like I said I feel a pull to her. I can at least let her feed me an apology dinner.

When I get to her place, I knock on the door and wait. When she doesn't answer, I walk around the deck to the back and see her sitting in the chair looking out at the lake. The sun shines on her, giving her an almost angelic appearance. She has sunglasses on blocking my view of her eyes, but the strapless sundress she has on shows off that sexy body that she has no idea that I've seen.

I move a step closer and she hears me, turning her head in my direction. I smile and walk over to her. "I knocked first."

"I'm sorry, I didn't hear. Would you like something to drink?" she asks, going to stand up.

"No, I'm good right now, thanks," I say, resting my hand on hers to have her sit back down.

I feel a bit awkward. I've been with plenty of women, but never without the intention of getting them in my bed. I don't exactly know what to discuss if it doesn't include bedroom talk.

"Wyatt, I really am sorry for the way I treated

you. I don't want you to think that is the kind of person I am," she says with sadness in her voice.

"Well, what kind of person are you?" I ask, generally interested in her response.

"If you would have asked me that a few months ago, I would have said a lawyer who wants to take the world by storm. Now, I'm not so sure anymore."

I look at her, but she never turns her attention away from the lake. "What changed?"

I know all too well how she's feeling because that's how her arrival to town is starting to make me feel. She has me questioning everything I thought I believed, and I don't understand any of it. Maybe if she tells me what changed for her, it will give me a little insight into what the hell is going on with me.

"Honestly?" She finally looks at me and I nod my head. "The clock," she says and smirks.

"The clock? What the hell does that mean?" I ask with a chuckle.

She turns her body to face me and smiles. "The ticking of the clock. It makes you realize time is passing and the longer it ticks, the more time passes. It made me realize that I have all this time passing me by and I wasn't doing anything with it.

I worked, ate, slept, has a few boring relationships, and no life at all. I want to do something with my life, but I'm not sure what it is. I know it sounds ridiculous. I shouldn't be boring you with this stuff. I should be sitting on some therapist's couch."

The more she spoke though, the more intrigued I became. She's on a quest to find herself and even though I think I'm probably the last thing she needs in her life, I want to help her.

"It's not ridiculous. Do you not want to be a lawyer anymore?"

"No, I love being a lawyer. I'm just not sure I want it to consume my life anymore."

"All right, well maybe when you go back home, you should throw that clock away," I joke hoping to lighten the mood a bit.

She laughs and stands up. "Maybe I will. I'm going to get a drink. Are you sure you don't want one?"

I tell her I'll take a water and she goes inside to get it. When she comes back outside, she has a platter with some fruit on it and our drinks. She places it all down before she sits.

"I will make burgers for dinner, but figured we could snack for a bit."

It's quiet for a few minutes while we just enjoy

the warm evening, but she said something earlier that has me curious. "Kendra, you said you had boring relationships. Why were they boring?"

She laughs and shakes her head. "Wyatt, you don't want to hear about that."

Normally, she's right, I wouldn't want to hear it. I shouldn't want to hear it from her, but damn it, I want to know. "Actually, I do."

"It's kind of embarrassing," she says shaking her head.

"Embarrassing? Well now you have to tell me."

"Well, the guys I've been with are boring. They don't enjoy going out, drinking more than two fingers worth of scotch, or even watching TV. Reading the newest law books, working, and a good cigar were things that held their interest. See, boring. What about you? What have your last relationships been like?" she asks, popping a grape into her mouth.

"Damn you are a lawyer, deflecting off the original question. Good thing for you I pay attention. Nothing you said is embarrassing. Boring as fuck, yes. Embarrassing, no. So what are you leaving out?"

Her eyes divert from mine and she shrugs her

shoulders and that's when it hits me. "The sex. They all sucked in bed. I'm right, aren't I?"

"Maybe."

"Totally."

"Ugh. Yes all right, that's exactly it," she says, covering the look of embarrassment on her face.

I pull her hands away and hold them while I grin at her. "Nothing embarrassing about that. Sometimes you just don't connect with a person."

It's been the opposite for me. I've had sexual satisfaction, but nothing else. No substance. I know it is mainly because of my lack of trust with women, though. I've never allowed myself to get close to anyone and I guess kind of like her, I've been filling that lonely void too, but with sex. I'm good at keeping my feelings out of any situation. I've been doing it most of my life. And up until I met her, I was fine with it.

Now, I'm starting to question everything, too.

CHAPTER EIGHT

KENDRA

IS it weird that I let him in? I shouldn't have. I should have pushed him away. But after hearing his side of the story, I've come to enjoy having him around. He's different from most guys.

Just the simple touch of his hand on mine and I feel my body come to life. Definitely something I haven't felt in a long time. So long in fact that I forgot what it felt like.

Wyatt carries on a conversation with me like he's generally interested in what I have to say; if he's not, he sure as hell plays the part well. It's things like this that I crave. Things like this that I miss. Things like this that a woman needs. I need.

As much as he wants to hear my story, I want to hear his. I want to hear about his time in Afghanistan. About all the war and things that he probably doesn't open up about. He hasn't told me anything and even though I only gave him a little, it's the biggest part.

"Wyatt, I answered you so now your turn. Tell me about your time overseas."

He takes a deep breath and lets it out ever so slowly. "I don't really talk about it much."

"I'd like for you to talk to me about it."

He smiles. "Why don't you ask me anything else, and one day I'll tell you about my time over there."

I can see the hurt and pain in his eyes, so I try to lighten the mood. "Okay, so what have your past relationships been like?"

This is truly a question that I want the answer to because my mind is all over the place with it. Wondering if he's had anything serious or just slept around.

Quirking his lip, he gives me a wink. "I don't think you really want to hear that."

Oh, how wrong he is. "Come on, you

promised. It's only fair." I pout, even going as far as to jut my lip out.

Chuckling, he reaches over and rests his hand on mine and I feel the sparks. "How about you get to know me a little more before we dig into my past relationships?"

Part of me is disappointed, but part of me is relieved. I'd like to know why he has the reputation he does. He likes to sleep around, that much I know for sure. Although I'd like to hear why.

On the other hand, I'm starting to like him, and if I know how many women he's been with or how he treated them, I may feel differently.

"Fair enough."

"Would you like to help me with dinner," he asks as I stand up.

"Okay." I smile.

For the next forty minutes, we work side by side in the kitchen and at the grill. It feels so natural, so normal, like this is something that couples do every day. Although I feel like it is so much more because I have had no one cook with me probably since my freshman year of college.

I'm enjoying the company, the laughs we are having about our different cooking styles, and the simple touches we share. We aren't a couple, but this is what I feel like I've been missing out on.

The little things.

Wyatt seems to enjoy himself as well. He's so much more relaxed than I've seen him yet. At the bar, he seems to be on edge. Like he's always "on". Always performing for or in pursuit of female attention. Our only other interaction was him trying to prove to me that he wasn't the asshole I was making him out to be.

I like this side of him. It's carefree, fun, and easygoing. I really want to get to know *this* Wyatt better.

After we eat, we sit on the deck and enjoy the cool evening breeze. It's now dark out and for some reason, it feels more intimate to me. I'm sure it's all in my mind considering the last few hours have made me realize how much I not only want but need a different life. I need a connection.

"Kendra, would you like to take a walk by the lake?" He stands up, holding his hand out to me.

I place my hand in his and he pulls me up. He leads us to a secluded spot on the lake that I've never noticed before. He doesn't let go of my hand as we duck under low-hanging trees through a narrow path that leads into what I can only describe as a grotto.

I let go of his hand and twirl around slowly, taking it all in. We are completely surrounded by a canopy of trees, the low-hanging moon peeking through the branches. The soft breeze whispers across the lake and small ripples lap at the shore.

"Wyatt, this is stunning," I whisper.

"It definitely is."

When I turn around to face him, I notice that he's watching my every move. The way he is looking at me, with the moonlight radiating off his deep brown eyes full of lust, has me squeezing my legs together.

I can't help but stare at him as he slowly walks toward me. My heart beats rapidly in my chest and my breath hitches in my throat. At this moment, although I'm not exactly sure what will happen, I feel a part of me come back to life.

"When's the last time you've visited here?" he asks me. "How come this is the first time I've seen you in years?"

"My career keeps me really busy and the last time I took a pause, three years had flown by."

"What about your parents? You haven't seen them in years?"

"They come to the city during Christmas for the Rockettes Show at Radio City Music Hall. I see them then. I guess Malik doesn't talk about me much."

"You know how it is. We only talk about family stuff when there's a problem. We don't do a lot of small talk. Men are simple creatures."

I giggle. "Yes, you are."

"This is a beautiful place, and your parents have only made it better with their structural improvements. Maybe you should visit more."

"Yeah," I say almost breathlessly. "Maybe I should."

Wyatt runs his knuckles down my cheek, and I involuntarily lean into his touch, my eyes drifting closed at the intimate gesture. He lifts my chin so that I am looking into his eyes.

"Kendra, I've never wanted to kiss someone as badly as I want to kiss you right now," he says, licking his lips.

I feel so desired looking at the moonlight reflecting in his heated eyes. I swallow and poke out my tongue to wet my lips.

"Kiss me," I whisper.

CHAPTER NINE

KENDRA

WYATT LEANS FORWARD and presses his lips to mine, and I melt into his arms. I wrap my arms around his neck and he licks the seam of my lips, seeking entrance. I open my mouth to him and when our tongues connect; I feel a fire burn throughout my whole body.

Unable to control myself, I moan as he sinks his fingers into my hair. He deepens the kiss, and I can't believe the reaction my body is having to him. It's overwhelming, yet I want so much more.

This kiss is not what I expected; it's slow, sweet and sensual. Almost like he is trying to express himself to me silently, and I am more than happy to listen.

Breaking the kiss, we both try to catch our breaths while searching each other's eyes. "I've wanted to do that since you walked into Gail's."

Wyatt leans forward and presses a soft kiss to my lips before pulling me into his arms. I rest my head on his chest as he rubs my back, and I can't help but smile.

He pulls me down to sit with him on the soft grass. Then he places me between his legs, my back to his chest and wraps his arms around me.

"Did you create this?" I ask, looking around at the grotto. I don't remember anything like this as a kid.

He kisses the top of my head and I feel him nod. "I did."

"It's stunning," I say looking around again. "I'm sure this has been a big hit with the ladies."

The minute the words leave my mouth, Wyatt's body stiffens, and I regret them.

"I'm sorry, it's none of my business who you've brought here. I shouldn't have said that."

"Kendra, you are the first person I've ever brought to my grotto."

Hearing him say it shocks me, and I turn my head to look at him.

"When I first moved here, I wanted to be anywhere else, but here. My dad told me to explore, and maybe I'd find something that would make me want to stay. Looking around the lake, I noticed all these trees and thought it would be amazing to be able to hide away in them. A place to escape to. It took a lot of work and many years, but knowing what it would look like when I was done, made moving here a little easier."

It breaks my heart knowing he was so sad to leave New York, yet I feel like he is opening up to me. I'll admit, I like it.

"Why did you need to move here?" I ask, placing my hands over his, trying to give him a bit of comfort.

"My mom walked out on my dad and me. I didn't realize it at the time because I was too busy being a teenager, but my dad needed this move. It was his way of moving on. At the time he gave me a choice to stay in New York with family. He didn't want to force me to move, but I'm so glad I did. He needed me and the move turned out to be one of the best decisions of my life. I love it here."

"Oh Wyatt, I'm so sorry about your mom. Malik never really talked about it."

"I'm not surprised. Not something I wanted broadcasted all over the village."

I don't know what else to say. He's giving me an insight into a piece of his life and it makes me feel closer to him. Wanting to change the subject because the sad voice I hear lets me know he doesn't enjoy visiting that part of his life. I suppose no one wants to talk about their mom abandoning them. So I decide to move the conversation in a different direction.

"So, do you enjoy working construction? It looks like you work with a fun bunch of guys."

He chuckles and squeezes me a little tighter. I think it's his way of thanking me for changing the subject.

"I do like my job, especially because ninety-nine percent of the time I work here at the resort. Malik and I are friends with most of the guys. They're a great group." He chuckles again, saying, "Well, most of the time they are."

We sit in the grotto and I listen to stories of what it was like once he moved here and we laugh at all the trouble he caused. I tell him what's been going on in New York and how much I loved coming here for the summers. The conversation is easy. Like talking to an old friend. It's so crazy I never noticed him as more than my brother's friend before.

Somehow we end up laying down, and I don't even mind the feeling of the grass and dirt on my skin. That's probably because my body is too focused on the solid, muscular chest I'm resting my cheek on. Even as we just lay here in silence, I feel there is an undeniable connection happening.

Wyatt surprises me when he moves, rolling me onto my back. He doesn't say a word just takes in my face in his hands before leaning forward and claiming my lips. This kiss differs from the first. It's hard, rough, and commanding. It makes my pussy ache with need, a feeling I'd forgotten about, but now it's a sensation I suddenly crave.

He breaks the kiss and puts his hands on either side of my face. "What the hell are you doing to me," he whispers before claiming my lips again.

I wish I had an answer for him, but I'm asking myself the same thing.

That was a kiss for the ages.

CHAPTER TEN

WYATT

WAKING UP THE NEXT MORNING, I have a
smile on my face remembering yesterday. It was
the best time I've ever had with a woman. We
talked, laughed, and got to know each other.... and I
actually gave a fuck.

When I brought her to my outdoor hangout, I'll
admit I was nervous. It's special to me, and I've
never shared it with anyone before. It's a place I
like to go to escape, but there was something about
the way I felt with Kendra that encouraged me to
take her there.

Going to work was not what I wanted to do. Running over to Kendra's, now *that* I was willing to do in a heartbeat. The kiss we shared last night was the most real thing I've ever experienced with a woman. I felt like we were connecting and not just in a sexual way.

Even though I wanted to spread her legs apart and fuck her senseless on that grass, I refused to even let it get to that point. I want her to like me, trust me, respect me. If I had slept with her last night, even if she was the one who initiated it, I was afraid she'd hate me. Plus, there's one major factor I have given little consideration. What will Malik think?

This is all so new and confusing to me, and right now, the only thing I want is to spend more time with her. Lucky for me, last night before I left her place, I asked her if I could take her somewhere after work. After another kiss, she said yes, so when I finish work today I will see her.

WORK IS ALMOST over and I'm relieved. I'm so damn distracted and the guys are noticing. They've been riding my ass to find out how dinner went, and I just keep saying fine. This is not appeasing them though.

"Something about her looks familiar," Todd says.

I swallow hard. I haven't told them who she is yet. It's only a matter of time before they figure it out or find out. She looks nothing like Malik, thank God, but her last name is a dead giveaway. Once they find that out, I'm toast.

"Did you kiss her?" I turn to look at Todd disapprovingly and he smirks. "What," he says, laughing.

"You act like a damn chick," I reply and shake my head with a smirk.

"Chick with a dick." We both burst out laughing.

"You're a fucking idiot." I turn back to the sheetrock I'm hanging and start screwing it in place.

"So did you?" he asks, standing right next to me. "I mean she sought you out and apologized. What woman does that unless she gives a shit?"

"Holy shit. Yes all right, I kissed her. No, I didn't go any further. Happy," I say completely fed up with the non-stop questions.

"Who sounds like a whining chick now?

Damn." He walks away laughing and I flip him off before getting back to work.

When we finally leave for the day, I go home and shower before making sandwiches. I pack up everything I need and head over to Kendra's. Like the chick that Todd said I sounded like, my stomach flips and turns the closer I get to her place. What the hell? I'm getting soft like ice cream.

I knock on her door and she opens it almost immediately. The air is sucked out of my lungs when I see how beautiful she looks. She's wearing a coral-colored sundress with her hair in a windswept updo with pieces that have fallen out framing her face. The exposed skin of her neck is begging for my touch, and it takes all my willpower to keep from carrying her to the bedroom. What gets me the most is the sexy smile she's wearing. Tonight is going to be hard. Literally.

"You look stunning," I say, moving in to kiss her. She wraps her arms around my neck and runs her fingers into my hair as I deepen the kiss. She lets out a soft moan, and I need to break the kiss because my hardened cock has other things in mind.

Smiling she says, "You look great too. So what are we doing?"

"Get your stuff and I'll show you."

She gets into my beat-up pickup truck, and I drive the short distance to one of my favorite open fields. Looking over at me she raises her eyebrows. "Well, this is more clear," she says causing us both to laugh.

"We are going to have a picnic." I open the door and look back over at her. "Come on."

After getting the blanket and picnic basket out of the bed of my truck, I grab her hand and lead her out into the field. We get to a spot that has the tall grass pressed down, probably from kids laying out here earlier, and I lay the blanket down. We sit down and she looks around.

"You know I spent so much of my childhood here and I don't remember any of this. How is that possible?"

"I think we are good at only holding onto the memories we treasure. Obviously, it wasn't the grounds you treasure." I wink at her reaching into the basket to pull out the sandwiches and pasta salad.

"You're right. It's the time I spent with my parents out of the city. They weren't too busy to play with me here," she says, resting her hands behind her. "We were happier here."

"Kind of sounds like what you are trying to avoid." I raise my eyebrows and grin.

She sits up quickly and looks more pissed off than I thought she would. *Crap.*

"What the hell is that supposed to mean?"

"Kendra, I meant nothing by it. You said all you used to do was work, but now you are taking time for yourself. Maybe that's something you need to do more often. That's all I meant," I say, hoping I didn't just fuck up our night.

She blows out a breath and leans back again. "No, you're right. Damn it, I never saw it like that, but that's exactly what I was becoming, my parents when we lived in the city."

She jets out her lower lip and says, "Don't let me become my parents, Wyatt."

We both chuckle and I climb on top of her, laying her onto her back. I kiss her lips, nipping on her bottom one. "You don't need me for that. You were fixing it anyway. That's why you're here."

Cupping my face in her hands, she smiles at me. "Is it weird to say that I feel this connection to you?"

"Thank fuck it's not just me," I say before crashing my lips to her. She runs her hands down my back, such a simple touch, but it makes me want to slam into her. I slowly drag my hand down her chest letting it lightly skim her tit.

She bucks her hips and breaks the kiss. "Oh God, Wyatt," she moans cocking her head back giving me access to her neck. I kiss down her neck, nipping every so often. I suck on the spot where shoulder connects, and she digs her nails into my back, letting me know she loves what I'm doing to her.

I kiss a path down her chest to the valley of her breasts and seeing the tops of ample tits spilling out of her dress is too much.

I pull away and sit back on my heels, running my hands through my hair. "Kendra, if I keep going we will end up fucking right here on this blanket."

She snaps her head up to look at me and the lust I see in her eyes makes my already hard cock harder. "Wyatt, it's been longer than I can remember since someone has made me feel like this."

Embarrassment colors her face before she covers it with her hands. This is a different Kendra. In the courtroom, she may be a badass, but under me, she's a novice. There's something about that I like.

She runs her fingertips along my chest in what

I think is an attempt to get me to move forward. Oh fuck, she is killing me. I lay on top of her and link her hands in mine.

"As badly as I want you right now, the sun is shining and we aren't exactly secluded here," I say looking around. "If you want to go back to my place or your place, I have no problem with it."

"Let's eat first and see how the rest of the night goes. Is that all right?" she suggests, pressing her hands against my chest as she leans forward to sit up.

"Anything you want is fine by me."

We eat in silence, and I look around the field thinking back. "Kendra?" She turns to look at me trying to force a smile. "If you were any other girl, I wouldn't have thought twice about fucking you in this field, shit I've done it countless times." I take a deep breath, and she looks at me confused.

"Uh, thanks?"

"Let me finish. There is something about you, Kendra. I don't know what it is, but I don't want to just sleep with you. I want something more. I know it sounds ridiculous because everyone should want that before they sleep together, but I never have."

I run my hands through my hair and groan.

"Shit, this is all coming out wrong. I'm probably scaring you off with every word I say."

She laughs and surprises the shit out of me when she climbs onto my lap. "Wyatt, when was your last serious relationship?"

Oh fuck, come on. My dick is brick hard.

"Honestly?"

"No, lie to me," she says, rolling her eyes.

I chuckle and search her eyes. "Never," I admit, whispering.

She sits back a bit to gauge my reaction and when she realizes I'm telling the truth, she looks into my eyes. "How is that possible?"

"I never wanted one before." I can't believe I am telling her all of this.

"But you do now?" she asks.

"I know that I don't want to just sleep with you and say goodbye afterward. I can't do that with you. I won't."

She smiles after my admission. "Will you tell me about your time overseas?"

"Is it important?"

"I think so. It's part of who you are and you don't talk about it. Makes me wonder why."

I suck in a breath and let it out slowly. "There

isn't much to tell," I say, stalling for a way to tell her some of my most horrible memories are of that place.

"Were you scared?"

"Every day," I tell her the truth because it was one of the most frightening things I've ever experienced.

I was in a specialized Army division called Overwatch. They gave us some of the more difficult assignments and I saw things that I wouldn't wish on my own worst enemy.

Keeping our country safe is not for the faint of heart. Not knowing if you will live or die at any moment. Watching friends get hurt and watching some die was enough to make me want to come home and never return.

"Are you glad to be back?" she asks me.

"Absolutely," I sigh. "Listen, I know I'm not telling you much, but believe me, Kendra, war isn't all it's cracked up to be. There are no heroes in war. There's no happiness. We just all go over there and try to complete our missions, try to survive, and try to keep as many of us alive as we can. I will never forget the men I fought with. They'll always be there for me."

A look crosses her face I've never seen before, and it's sexy as fuck. "I'm glad you're back safe."

"Me too."

The heat grows between us.

"Take me home, Wyatt." She stands up and starts packing everything away. "Now."

CHAPTER ELEVEN

KENDRA

MY NERVES ARE TINGLING as I pack everything up. Hearing Wyatt tell me about his time overseas explains so much. I think he lives his life every day as if it were his last. Sleeping with all the women he has. Creating a sanctuary at the grotto to find a bit of peace. I think I understand him more. He's wounded. He's guarded. He's a man that I find myself wanting to hold and never stop.

When he told me he wanted something more with me, I didn't know what to say. This is all moving at the speed of light. Sure, he's not a total stranger, but in many ways he is. I know Wyatt the scrawny kid. Friend of my brother. Not Wyatt the hot, military man.

The crazy part is that now I think that I want more with him, too. I at least want the time to explore what "more" could look like. I can't let go of this attraction for him. It won't stop. It's like this fire has been burning since I first saw him in the bar. God, I'm acting like a horny teenager.

Wyatt didn't say a word as we packed up and still nothing on the short drive home. I'm hoping it's because he's as turned on as I am; I can hardly think straight. My body is burning with need, a fire he started and only he can put out. A desire that runs so deep I don't know how I'll ever survive from it.

We pull up to my place and he throws the truck in park then turns to look at me. "Kendra, are you sure about this? I don't want you to feel like I'm rushing you."

"This is you rushing?" I ask playfully. "Because you've barely touched me," I say, opening the door and climbing out.

I walk up the steps to the small trailer and look

back over my shoulder. He winks playfully as we step inside and close the door. Suddenly, closed in the small space just me and Wyatt, I feel nervous. He's known for his promiscuous ways, and while I'm no prude, I'm just concerned that I won't live up to the playful romps in the sack he's used to.

While my partners have always been cautious and boring, the kind of women Wyatt's been with are sex kittens. At least that's what I imagine. I know just from kissing him that sex will be mind-blowing and he will be expecting the same.

He lifts my chin up, forcing me to look at him. "What's going on in that brain of yours?"

I shake my head nervously as he searches my eyes.

"Listen, if we want something to come of this, you need to be honest with me. Are you having second thoughts?" he asks.

I blow out a breath and pick at the hem of my dress. "No second thoughts. It's just.."

"Your brother?"

"Wait, what? Malik? No, he has nothing to do with this."

"Then what?"

I pause for a second to build up my courage.

"Well, the guys I'm normally with are, well, nothing like you. And I know I'm not the kind of woman you are usually with. What if I can't, you know, do the kinds of things that you're used to?"

Without a word, he grabs my hand and leads me to the bedroom. He flips on the light and stands in front of my bed. Pulling his shirt over his head, he drops it to the floor and my body starts to feel the slow burn again, seeing his muscular chest.

Still without saying a word, he unbuttons his jeans and lets them pool around his ankles. I can't move. I can't breathe. Seeing him with nothing on but his black boxer briefs and a smoldering look in his eyes has my nipples pebbling under my dress.

Wyatt's body is something I didn't actually know existed in real life. No one I have ever been with has been half as sexy. He has the body of someone who works out, takes good care of himself, and someone who cares what others think. It's hard. It's chiseled. It's spectacular. Honestly, it puts mine to shame. He makes me want to suck in my gut a little tighter.

I haven't said a word or moved an inch. If I do, this fantasy might end and I sure as hell don't want that. He moves a little closer and I look into his heated eyes. He lifts his left eyebrow.

"My clothes are off, Kendra. Why the fuck aren't yours?"

With my heart pounding in my chest, he watches me with a need I've never seen before. I silently grab the hem of my sundress and pull it over my head, leaving me exposed to him in nothing but my teal satin strapless bra and panties.

"Gorgeous," he exhales.

The way he is taking in my body, raking his eyes over every inch, makes me feel wanted and desired. He takes the last few steps and stands right in front of me. I feel so out of my element considering I'm used to being in bed, taking off my clothes while under the covers and keeping my body hidden most of the time. I feel like that would never be an option with Wyatt, not with the way he licks his lips before he reaches his hand out and touches my cheek.

"You're right. You aren't like any of the women I usually have sex with. You are so much more," he whispers before presses his lips to mine.

His words sink in, and I know that he feels something for me, something more than just sexual. He pulls me flush against him and when my skin touches his, my body nearly goes up in flames. His hard chest against me and muscular arms wrapped around me are my undoing. I moan and run my hands down his body feeling every groove and valley, feeling a bit more confident after his words.

"Don't worry about the types of things I'm used to doing in bed, Kendra. I got this. I got you."

Wyatt lowers me to the bed and allows me to position myself before he climbs on top of me. "I've never wanted someone more than I want you right now. Don't forget that for a second. You understand me?"

I'm not sure if I'm supposed to answer him or if that was a rhetorical question until he speaks again. "I asked you if you understand?"

Wetness rushes between my legs.

"Yes, Wyatt."

He claims my lips fiercely before kissing a path down to my breasts. My chest heaves and my breasts beg to be touched, so when he cups them I toss my head back. Reaching around me he unfastens my bra and tosses it behind him. He takes in my breasts for a minute before looking at my face.

"Fucking beautiful."

Bending his head he pays homage to my breasts, awakening a feeling in me that has been dormant for far too long. Continuing his exploration of my body, he makes his way down to the top of my panties. Hooking his fingers inside, he pulls them down my legs and they join my bra on the floor. Pushing my legs wider apart, he lets out a growl that vibrates through my body. My nipples are hard and my pussy is dripping with need and watching him take in my naked body is so erotic.

"Wyatt," I whisper, and he snaps his head to mine.

"You're breathtaking. Everything about you is perfection. Now I need to see what you look like when I make you come," he says before I feel his hot breath blow across my pussy. He runs his fingers from my opening to right before my clit. "You are so wet, do you have any idea how fucking hot that is? How fucking hot you are?"

I squeeze my eyes shut, letting the feelings run through my body, unsure of how to answer him. Slowly he pushes a finger inside me, and the sensation when he enters is so strong that if he wasn't holding my thighs down I'd have shot off the bed.

Adding another finger he begins to finger fuck

me and my world tilts on its axis. Just the feel of his talented fingers has my body burning with a desire I've never known. Nothing matters at the moment, nothing but the two of us and the way we make each other feel.

He licks with precision at my pussy as he continues working me over with his magical fingers, and I fist the blanket in my hands tossing my head back.

"Oh God, Wyatt," I shout when his tongue makes impact with my clit.

He licks at it with a speed I didn't know a tongue could achieve and I feel my orgasm on the brink. It's been so long since I've been given one, but it's not a feeling you forget. He picks up the speed, and the force of his finger fucking as he sucks on my clit has my orgasm ripping through me so hard and fast, I wasn't even expecting it.

"Shit!" I shout and moan while I ride out the strongest orgasm I've ever experienced.

He removes his fingers but continues to lick at my sensitive pussy causing my orgasm to go on and on. He finally climbs up my body and grabs a hold of my face, searching my eyes. "Fuck that was hot," is all he says before kissing me and allowing me to taste myself.

I've never tasted myself before, and I'm surprised that the salty flavor actually turns me on. Maybe it's the fact that it's on him or the erotic images of what he's just done, but I grab onto his hair holding him to me.

When we pull away from the kiss he says, "I need to fuck you."

He stands up and grabs a condom out of his jeans before stepping out of his boxers. His dick juts out in front of him, thick and hard, making me excited for what will happen next. He climbs back on the bed and sits on his heels, watching me while he rolls the condom over the sexist penis I've ever seen. A dick that will be inside me soon, connecting us even more.

He lies on top of me and I feel the head of his dick at my entrance and I start to worry. I know he said that he's got this, but I'm once again nervous that I won't be able to satisfy him. Especially not in the way like he just did for me.

He hasn't broken eye contact and kisses me quickly before speaking a whisper across my lips.

"You are still okay with this, right?" I nod my head and he grins.

"Good. I'll go as slow or as fast as you want. I

may be in charge of the pleasure, but you're in charge of the tempo."

"Okay," I quietly sigh in relief.

As he pushes into me, I accidentally dig my nails into his biceps. On top of the fact that I haven't had sex in months, Wyatt is bigger than I've ever had.

"Damn, I'm not even fully seated inside of you yet. Am I hurting you?"

"I'm fine."

I look into his eyes, begging him to continue. He must understand what I need because he pushes in halfway and stops.

"Feels okay?"

I nod my head because forming words right now is an impossible feat. He stretches me out and fills me in a way no man ever has before. He pushes the rest of the way in and stills again.

"You're so beautiful, Kendra," he says before he starts moving.

The feeling is delicious and all-consuming having this beautiful man on top of me, wrapped around me, and inside of me. The more he moves, the more relaxed I feel and start moving with him. Meeting him thrust for thrust, listening to the noises we are both making, makes me want him that much more.

"Oh God, Wyatt, I need more."

Without hesitation, he picks up his speed and my body crests with desire. I've never had my body react this way to a man, and it's not just my body, but my heart has joined in.

I can't deny it. I won't deny it. I really am starting to like this man. He is both strong and soft, light and dark, chivalrous and pompous. I'm completely and shamelessly drawn to him like a moth to a flame.

Whatever is happening between us isn't initially what I was seeking when I came home to Day's Ranch. I didn't know what I wanted. I thought it was simple, friviolous, fun. This is not that. This is way more than that. God knows this is not exactly going to make Malik jump for joy. He never shared really well, but I won't let that stop this from happening either.

Hell, a connection like this comes around once in a blue moon. So while the practical side of me wants to pause and analyze every decision I'm making, there is another part of me telling me to relax. To allow Wyatt to control every part of me. I need him to. I want him to control me. To make me feel so fucking good. Because he already does, every time we're together.

"Kendra, your pussy is so fucking tight," he growls deeply. "Give me more."

Wyatt fucks me so hard that my body moves inches up the bed with each thrust. My head almost hitting the headboard. I reach my hands over my head, holding onto it as he slams inside me. Never slowing down, he continues to thrust in and out of me bringing me closer and closer to what I'm sure will be an even more powerful orgasm than the last.

"I'm so close," I moan shamelessly.

"I know, baby, I feel you," he says, reaching his hand down and rubbing my clit. "Let me get you there even faster."

My entire body reacts. My entire body lights up like a firecracker exposed. Lifting off the ground and exploding into an array of colors and sounds. So beautiful in all its glory and never fading until the last ember has had its moment to shine free.

Tugging on his hair, I scream out his name as my release crashes over me, pulling me under. He thrusts into me a few more strides before he growls my name when his orgasm finds him. He grunts into my ear, saying my name over and over.

"Damn, Kendra."

We lay holding each other tightly while we return to our bodies. "Wyatt, that was ... I don't know what that was."

He chuckles and says, "A spiritual experience."

I roll my eyes. "You think very highly of yourself."

"I think very highly of you." He starts to tickle my side.

"Aah! Stop it."

"I remember you being ticklish when we were kids."

"How do you remember that? I didn't think any of Malik's friends were paying attention to me."

"You were always memorable, Kendra. But now you're unforgettable."

An hour later we are still lying in bed, naked, my body pressed against his. We can't seem to get enough of touching each other. He's rubbing small circles on my back and I'm tracing his muscular chest. I could stay like this for a lifetime and be happy. Of course, I'm getting way ahead of myself.

"Kendra, can I ask you something?"

I move my hand to his face and say, "Anything."

"Have you ever been in love before," he asks looking at me with vulnerable eyes.

That's a tough question for me right now. If he'd asked me a few weeks ago, I would have said yes. Now, I don't know.

"Well, I thought I was once or twice, but I'm not so sure anymore." He gives me a puzzled look and I try to find the right words. "I think to be in love, you need to give your whole heart to the other person. I think you need to have complete trust, understanding, and devotion. You need a connection both physically and emotionally. I thought along the way that maybe I'd found the right guy, turns out I hadn't."

He nods his head but doesn't reply. I wonder if maybe I've said too much, but he said he wanted honesty.

"Have you ever been in love?"

"No," he says without even a second thought.

He says it so tersely; I wonder what the story is behind it. Does the thought of being in love turn him completely off? Does he even believe that love exists?

I want to ask more about his emphatic no, but then again I'm not sure I want to know the answer; so for now, I just leave it. Especially because I'm laying naked across his body after earth-shattering sex.

After Wyatt brings me to another orgasm with his masterful tongue, I feel myself being pulled under to sleep. The last thought I have before I am dragged under is, I think I could love him.

CHAPTER TWELVE

WYATT

I WAKE up tangled around Kendra and smile. I know it's a little fucked up, but I've never spent the night with a woman before. This is a first for me, because I always ask them politely to leave.

Everything that is happening and every decision I'm making with Kendra is the complete opposite of the guy I usually am. The way she felt in my arms while we had sex and as we lay in bed last night, it made me think I could be falling for her. I didn't want her to leave. It felt right.

I asked her if she'd ever been in love, and as she

defined what that means to her, I felt that is exactly what is happening to me. It shocked me at first but then filled me with a sense of total understanding.

The idea of being with one woman was something I never wanted, something I totally avoided, until now. This just might be me ... falling.

Kendra stirs in her sleep, bringing me back to the present, and I decide to let her snooze while I go see if there is anything to make for breakfast. Getting out of bed as slowly as I can, I grab my boxers and jeans before leaving the bedroom. I slip them on, then check her fridge and cabinets for food. I decide to make pancakes and bacon and pull all the ingredients I need out.

Just as I'm plating everything, I feel Kendra's warm arms wrap around my waist. "Good morning," she says before placing a kiss on my back.

I spin around and pull her to me, loving the feel of her. I kiss her nose and smile. "Morning. How did you sleep, baby?"

"I slept great. Best sleep I've had in a long time," she says smiling back.

"My deep strokes put your ass to sleep, huh?"

She playfully slaps my arm. "Don't be crude, Wyatt."

"Are you hungry?" I ask while holding back a laugh.

We make our plates and go sit on the deck to eat. Even with her hair a mess and my t-shirt on (especially with my t-shirt on), she is breathtaking.

"Nice shirt," I say giving her a wink. "Looks good on you."

She throws her head back laughing and looks over at me. "Well, you left it here, so I thought I'd better use it. Plus, it's comfortable."

I grin and lean over to kiss her lips. "Keep it."

After we finish our breakfast, we clean up the mess and then settle on the deck with fresh coffee. Kendra has fallen silent, and I wonder what she's thinking about.

Just as I open my mouth to ask, she says, "Wyatt?" I raise my eyebrows and her cheeks get a hint of pink. "What happened the first night we met? The real story."

"Don't worry about it. It's forgotten now," I say. I don't want her to be embarrassed.

"Please, I need to know. Did I make a complete fool of myself?"

I rub the back of my neck and try to decide what to say, but when I notice the desperation on her face, I know I need to tell her the truth.

"Fine. Driving home from the bar, you kept fading in and out of consciousness. I wanted to get you home quickly, but I wasn't exactly sure if you were staying with your folks or at your own rental.

"So when we pulled into the resort entrance, Tony, the security guard at the front gate, phoned your mom and got your cabin number. You were moaning, and not in a good way," I say, giving her a wink, trying to lighten the situation. "When I pulled you out of the car, you threw up all over yourself."

She covers her face and shakes it. "Oh, my God. I'm so sorry."

I place my hand on hers and grin. "No need to apologize. Regardless of my attraction to you, you are my best friend's little sister. The least I could do was look out for you. So I brought you inside and undressed you, then cleaned you up.

"I didn't take off your bra and panties until I put my shirt on you, I swear. After that, you passed out. I sat on the edge of the bed to monitor you during the night. Make sure you didn't vomit in your sleep or something."

She searches my face and the look on hers makes everything worth it. It's a mixture of gratitude, surprise, and relief.

"You sat on my bed all night keeping vigil?"

"I wanted to make sure you were all right," I confess.

"Why would you do that? Just because I was Malik's sister?"

I shrug my shoulders and sip my coffee. "I thought that was why at first, but now I realize there was something about you, and it had nothing to do with you being Malik's sister. I felt drawn to you; I wanted to keep you safe. I felt like you were my responsibility. I still do."

Kendra moves over to me and straddles my lap. I rest my hands on her rounded firm ass and squeeze. She leans forward and captures my lips, getting the attention of my dick yet again. The longer and deeper the kiss, the harder I am getting. She pulls away and looks around before returning her gaze to me. She reaches down and tries to unbutton my jeans.

"Easy, Kendra, if you release the Kraken I won't be able to control myself," I warn her with a lustful smile.

She pulls the zipper down and stands up to free me from the confines of my jeans and boxers. Once the air hits my dick, I know I'm a goner. Sitting down she kisses and sucks on my neck, making it impossible for me to think of anything else but having her ride my cock. She looks at me with lust in her eyes and says, "I need you right now."

"Fuck yes, let's go," I say, waiting for her to stand up.

She doesn't though, she leans into my ear and whispers, "No, I want you to fuck me right here, right now."

Holy shit.

I reach into my pocket, thankful I brought a few condoms, and roll one over myself. I reach under the t-shirt she has on and cup one of her heavy breasts in my palm. I use the fingers on my other hand to play with one of her nipples. Rolling and pinching it in between my fingers. Squeezing and releasing pressure. Falling even harder for her as her hips begin to gyrate with need.

"Fuck, Kendra."

She stands just enough to sink down on my waiting cock. We both let out a moan and I sink my fingers into her ass. I nip her hardened nipples over the t-shirt and lightly smack her ass. I see pure ecstasy on her face as she tries to keep her eyes open.

"Ride me, baby."

Kendra tilts and rolls her hips—a bit unsure of herself—and I help guide her by pulling her toward me with my hands on her ass. Once she finds the perfect rhythm, it takes over my body. Her soft, tight pussy is sucking me and when she grips onto my shoulders and starts to really move, I'm done.

"Wyatt, oh God I'm so close already," she moans.

I meet her thrust for thrust and feel my balls tighten and a fire spread in my stomach. I won't last much longer.

"Whose pussy is this?" I ask with a guttural and possessive growl.

"Yours."

"Whose?"

"Yours, Wyatt."

"That's right, baby. Don't you fucking forget it."

I rub Kendra's clit and she lets out a sound of pure pleasure, followed by her pussy gripping me so tightly, we find our releases simultaneously.

"Look at me, Kendra. I need to see you," I manage to say.

When her eyes meet mine, I know in this

moment, that I've fallen. There is no denying it, or questioning it, or avoiding it.

For the first time in my life, it's as plain as the nose on my face.

I'm falling in love and this shit is something.

CHAPTER THIRTEEN

WYATT

AFTER A DAY OF EXPLORING, dinner, and of course another night of the best sex I've ever had, we are lying in bed. I have work in the morning, but that isn't going to keep me from spending the night with her. Hell, we only stay three minutes from each other. I will run home in the morning and get ready if I need to.

"Wyatt," she says, her voice full of sleep.

"What, baby?"

"You make me happy."

That's it. That's all she says before she passes

out, but it was a major admission. I make Kendra Collins happy.

"Baby, you make me happy too. Thank you for that," I say, knowing even if she hears me she won't remember in the morning, but I sure as hell will.

FOR THE NEXT FEW DAYS, the only time Kendra and I aren't together is when I'm working. As soon as I get off, I go to her place or she comes here. Tonight is Friday, and I'm looking forward to being with her all weekend. She is coming over here for dinner and then we will definitely be having dessert.

"What are your plans tonight? You want to meet up at the bar?" Todd asks.

"No, not tonight. I've got plans." I don't look at him and just continue to pack my stuff away.

"Oh really? Are you still seeing that hot chick from the bar? Is that where you've been all week?" he asks leaning up against the wall.

I stand up and cross my arms. "Kendra, her name is Kendra. And yes, I'm still seeing her and we have plans," I say, a bit annoyed that he keeps making light of the situation like I'm going to dump her at any minute for a new piece of ass.

He holds up his hands in a surrender gesture and backs away from me. I chuckle because I didn't even say it nasty.

"I'm just asking, man. I didn't realize that you had suddenly changed your ways. Never seen you date the same chick more than once. You can't blame a dude for being surprised. This isn't your normal M.O. "

I want to be pissed about his comment, but he is just saying what everyone else is thinking. I've noticed the stares and whispers when some of the town regulars see me with Kendra.

I personally don't give a shit; I just don't want it to bother her. Shaking my head, I finish packing up and tell the guys I'll see them Monday.

When I get home, Kendra is sitting on my steps. She looks beautiful with her hair in soft curls, a sexy black dress on, and her big smile. I jump out of my truck and walk over to her.

"Not that I'm not happy as hell to see you, but what are you doing here so early?" I ask as she stands up.

"Why don't we ever go out," she asks as soon as I reach her.

"What? We go out all the time. Yesterday we spent the day at the lake," I say, walking past her to open the door. I get in the door and she is right on my heels.

"Wyatt, that's not what I mean. Yes, we do a lot of things in the resort, at the lake, at the grotto– but why don't we ever go out to dinner or the bar?"

She gives me sad eyes, and I pull her to me.

"Kendra, why do you want to go out so bad? We'd only be rushing home to get under each other's clothes anyway," I say, trying to make light of the situation.

"Is that your favorite place to have me? In bed?"

"That is the craziest question you've ever asked me. Of course that's my favorite place to have you, but don't get it twisted. It's not the *only* place."

"Are you ashamed of me or something?"

I pull back and let go of her. I start to pace and rub the back of my neck, shocked that she would even think that. Wondering what I've done to make her even question this.

I turn around to face her and blow out a breath. "How could you ask that? You are the best thing to ever happen to me. You are beautiful, smart, funny, and sexy as fuck. It's me, all right. You don't notice the way people whisper or stare at us here. It would be worse in town. I just want to keep you safe from all that bullshit."

She wraps her hands around my neck before kissing my lips. My hands automatically land on her ass and she smiles.

"You don't give me enough credit, Mr. Drake. I am a damn good lawyer and I see it all. I see the looks and the snickers and the whispers... and guess what? I don't care. The person they think you are isn't the real you. I know that and that's what matters. Now, go shower and get dressed because we are going out to dinner and then to the bar. Show me the fuck off."

Damn, she's hot when she's all bossy, but she does not understand how badly this is going to end. "I think it's a bad idea, baby."

"That's fine because I wasn't asking. Go get ready," she says and kisses my lips.

Not wanting to argue with her, I do just as she says. I can't help but think of all the questions and comments that are going to be coming our way tonight, especially from my friends.

Hopefully, she is strong enough to handle it

because they will be relentless, especially at the bar. Right now, in the moment, I wish I had done a lot of things differently.

Because tonight is going to suck ass.

CHAPTER FOURTEEN

KENDRA

IT'S cute how Wyatt tried so hard to change my mind. He doesn't want to go out, and I know exactly why. He's slept with half the tourists and probably half of the female residents over twenty-one-years-old in this town and he thinks everyone making comments behind our backs will bother me.

The thing he doesn't get is that I'm a lawyer. I can handle anything thrown at me. I've had newspapers rip apart my ability of cases, clients give me threats if I lost a case, and even my bosses screaming at me.

The fact that he's slept around a lot and people talk about it, that doesn't bother me and it shouldn't bother him. He's a grown-ass man, and he's allowed to live his life whatever way he chooses to.

At dinner — which I'll admit he was nervous — he kept looking around the restaurant. Honestly, there were only a few people who were whispering about us. Now we are on our way to the bar and he looks even more nervous.

"Wyatt, I wish you'd relax and try to have fun."

He looks over at me for a second before focusing back on the road. "I'm not nervous. I'm just staying alert."

I burst out laughing and he shoots me a look. "I'm sorry, but what are you staying on alert for exactly?"

"Laugh all you want. Dinner was nothing compared to what it's going to be like at the bar."

"We met at the bar."

"Exactly my point. That's where all my friends are tonight, and they have been giving me a hard time as it is about you. I just don't want you thinking any less of me, all right," he says and my heart hurts at his defeated tone.

It almost makes me want to tell him to just

take us home, but no. I want to go out. I don't want to have to always hide in the grotto or the cabins.

"There is nothing that anyone can say or do that would make me think less of you. You've awakened a part of me I thought was dead. You make me laugh, you make my heart beat out of my chest, and the way you make me come... believe me, nothing they say will change the way I feel about you," I say, meaning every word and hoping it puts him at ease.

We pull into the parking lot of the bar and when he parks the truck; he turns to face me. "You like the way I make you come, huh," he says, grinning at me. "Now who's being *crude*."

I reach over and smack his chest and we both laugh. He holds my hand against his chest by his heart and says, "You feel that?" I nod my head and he continues.

"You are the reason my heart beats again. So, yes I worry that someone will say something that will disgust you, and you'll walk away. I'm not ready to lose you. Not when we just started."

I climb across the seat (which ain't easy with these hips) and straddle his lap. I kiss him passionately, hoping the silent affection shows how much he means to me. I pull back, rest my forehead on his, and say the scariest thing.

"You aren't going to lose me."

I kiss him again and this time when I break the kiss I say, "How about you tell me the worst things I could hear, that way you won't need to worry."

"I don't know. I just told you I think you'll be disgusted. Why would I risk it?"

I kiss his cheek and say, "Try me." I can see him warring with himself on whether to tell me or not, so I kiss his soft lips to let him know it's all right.

"Fine. Well first off, I've never talked to a woman after I slept with her. In fact, I've gone out of my way to avoid it. One time I had a threesome–" I try not to flinch. "And when we were done they started to fall asleep; I woke them both up and told them to leave."

"Okay."

"Another time I slept with a woman who was only separated from her husband. I think she may have even still lived with him. I didn't ask. I could go on and on about my questionable choices, but my point is that I've never been serious about anyone before.

"I've never been in a relationship, even as a

teenager. I've been selfish, and I didn't care if I hurt any of the women I slept with," he tells me, never once making eye contact. "I never even considered that they had feelings."

I'll admit I'm shocked by some of it, but it just makes me want to know one thing. "Why?"

"Why have I been a pig?"

"No, why haven't you been serious about anyone or in a relationship? Why wouldn't you care if you hurt them?" I ask generally confused. "Why do you treat women like you hate them?"

The guy he was just talking about is not the guy I know. In fact, he's the complete opposite.

"I love women, I respect women, but I've never trusted women. The one woman I trusted with my heart walked out on me and never looked back. All the women my dad fell for after the marriage dissolved left.

"The only experience I had with women as a kid was watching them walk away. I didn't want to be left behind, so I figured if I never got close to anyone, they could never hurt me. My time in the military only made it worse. I lost people. People who mattered to me. It made me even more guarded."

"I'm sorry, Wyatt."

"I know it's fucked up, but you asked for the truth," he says, and I can hear the shame in his voice. "So that's the truth."

I do the only thing I can to show him how much I appreciate his honesty and that I don't judge him for it. I unbutton his jeans then slip my hand into his boxers and grip his hard dick.

"Baby, what are you doing?"

"Showing you how much I care for you. How much I respect your honesty, and how turned on I am," I say pumping him in my hand.

"Honesty turns you on?" he smirks. "You're such a nerd, baby."

He pushes his jeans down just enough to allow his beautiful penis to be free and I climb off his lap and back into the passenger seat. Before he can even say anything else, I lean down and lick a path from his balls to the head of his dick.

He bucks forward slightly, and I take him in my mouth. I move my head up and down, taking as much of him as I can, loving the feel of him in my mouth.

"Fuck, Kendra," he hisses when I scrape my teeth on the back of his dick.

He fists his hands in my hair and rotates his hips. It's only spurring me on, and I want to make him come hard. The faster I suck his cock, the faster he moves his hips. He lets out a string of curses, and I smile around his cock, proud of my abilities. Reaching my hand down, I fondle his balls.

"Holy fuck. I'm not going to last, baby. Fuck," he growls.

I pick up my pace and within seconds I feel his balls tighten in my hands.

He lets out a loud moan and says, "Shit, Kendra, I'm going to come, take it all, baby. Fuck, take it all."

And that's just what I do when he finds his release. I swallow every drop he has to give and when I know he's done; I sit up licking my lips.

"That was hot," I say, looking into his sated eyes. "You liked it didn't you." I grin.

"Kendra?"

"What?"

"I love you," he says, looking directly into my eyes and what I feel like is my soul.

I know it's happened quickly; I know it makes no sense at all, but I'm starting to understand why I've been led back home. It was for this moment right here. To find Wyatt. To love Wyatt.

I know that he means what he just said to me. I

can feel it in my bones. He loves me, and I feel like the luckiest woman in the world because I feel exactly the same way.

I climb onto his lap and kiss him. "I love you too, Wyatt ."

We hold on to each other, blissfully happy. That is until someone bangs on the window, scaring the shit out of me and causing me to scream.

"What the fuck," Wyatt yells while rolling down his window. "Todd, what the fuck?"

"You've been sitting here for a while. I figured I better check on you. I can see I've interrupted, I'll just leave you to it," he says chuckling.

"Todd, get the fuck out of here before I kick your ass."

"Yeah, yeah. Finish up in there and come get a drink." He turns around and heads back to the bar.

"I'm so sorry he interrupted our moment. We can leave now," he says, gripping the side of my face for another kiss.

"Not a chance in Hell." I give him a quick peck. "You just told me you love me, so we need to celebrate."

He chuckles and shakes his head while fixing his jeans. "Anything you want, baby." He leans over and kisses my lips and pulls back to look into my eyes. "Anything," he whispers, causing goosebumps to break out all over my skin.

We enter the bar holding hands, and just like Wyatt feared all eyes are on us. I nudge him and nod my head toward the bar. I'll have a glass of wine, but that's it. No way am I getting trashed again.

He places our order with Gail and she looks at us with wide eyes but doesn't say a word. Within seconds Wyatt's friends are surrounding us.

"Well, who is this beauty?" One of his friends asks running his eyes over my body.

I lift my eyebrows and say, "I'm Kendra."

"You look so familiar." One of his other friend's comments. "Is this your first time visiting the resort?"

"No, my parents own the ranch."

There's dead silence around us. Every single one of Wyatt's friends is staring at me like I have two heads.

"You're Malik's sister?"

"Yes, do you know my brother?" I ask feigning ignorance.

They all stare at Wyatt for a moment and then focus back on me.

"Absolutely. Malik is one of our closest friends. He's mentioned you many times. The high-powered lawyer in Manhattan he's so proud of. I can't believe that none of us recognized you."

"I've changed a lot over the years," I admit.

"Yeah, the hell you have. You are way prettier than Malik." Everyone but Wyatt chuckles. I thank him, but he just continues. "When are you going to be done with Wyatt so you can come hang out with a real man?"

"Joe, that's it." Wyatt steps forward. "If you don't shut the fuck up, I will beat your ass right in the middle of this bar."

I guess Joe is afraid of Wyatt because he backs away with his hands up and goes looking for someone else to cause trouble with.

Another one of his friends, Todd, asks respectfully for him to talk for a moment, but Wyatt doesn't let go of my hand.

"You can say what you need to in front of Kendra."

He pauses for a moment as he appears to gather his thoughts then speaks. "Did you know this entire time that she was Malik's sister?"

"Yeah."

He scratches his head in confusion.

"So what are you doing, Bro'?"

"What do you mean?"

"Obviously this is more than a one-night thing for you, but did you tell him?"

"He's away."

"He's hunting and fishing down south. He's not in Antartica. They got cell phones there."

"I met his sister. That didn't seem like it warranted an emergency phone call."

"You are, and excuse me, Kendra, but you are *fucking* his sister. That warrants a phone call in my book."

I shift uncomfortably next to Wyatt. I haven't given my brother a second thought during this whole thing, but maybe I should have. This is more his town than mine. He lives and works with these people. Did I just break some sort of code by falling for his best friend? Will this mean trouble for Wyatt?

"Appreciate the concern, brother, but we will handle it. Let's just have a good time tonight."

Wyatt squeezes my hand to let me know he's got me. I squeeze his back.

"As long as you've got it handled, I'll mind my business. Nice to meet you again, Kendra."

"You too, Todd."

Gail hands us our drinks, and I take a sip looking around. It seems more alive tonight than it did last time I was here. Maybe it's just the fact that the last time I was here I was miserable and this time I'm in love.

In love?

I don't know how it happened so fast, but it did and I feel like I'm where I'm supposed to be. Being with Wyatt is so much more than what I thought I was looking for, and I can't think of a time I've been happier.

Once everyone got used to the idea that I'm Malik's little sister and that Wyatt and I are together, it ended up being a great night. We drank, danced, and laughed. It couldn't have been more perfect. Wyatt finally relaxed, and the love I saw when he looked at me was present all night, making my heartbeat steady in my chest.

When he asked if I was ready to leave, I nodded my head. I was so ready to go home and show him just how much I loved him because until Wyatt, I didn't know what true love was.

CHAPTER FIFTEEN

WYATT

"HELLO?"

"Hey, man."

"Wyatt? Hey, dude, what's up? Everything good?"

"Sick of hunting and fishing yet?"

"Naw, man. You know I could do this for another month if dad wanted to."

"Cool, glad you're having a good time."

"Bro', I love you and shit, but why are we chatting it up like you're my girl or something. My mom doesn't even call us when we're away. There's a reason dad and I have a no cell phone rule on these trips and I'm breaking it for this?"

I texted him our 911 code before I called, so he'd know to pick up.

"There's something I need to talk to you about."

"Better be good."

"Your sister came to visit your mom."

"Kendra's there? Damn! How long is she staying?"

"Don't know...thing is...she and I have been spending some time together."

There's a long pause then Malik finally speaks again.

"You taking care of her for me?"

"More than that."

There's another long pause.

"You better not be fucking her, Wyatt."

"More. Than. That."

"What more could there fucking be?"

"I'm in love with her."

"You've never loved a woman in your whole miserable life!"

"Exactly...that's why you should know that I'm serious if I'm telling you that I am in love with her."

He sighs heavily. "She's my sister, man."

"I know, and you are like family to me. I would never enter into this lightly. You have to know that."

"She loves you too?"

"Why did you say that like it's impossible?" I chuckle.

"I mean you're cute and shit, but Kendra's always been devoted to her work. I can't imagine that she's stopped being a lawyer long enough to even notice your ass."

"Well, things change."

"I guess they do."

"So I have your blessing?"

"You're always doing shit ass-backward, dude. You should have asked me for my blessing long before you touched her, but now that you have, yes. You have it. Just don't hurt her or then you're going to have a problem. A Collins family problem."

"Understood."

"Oh and Wyatt—"

"Yeah."

"I'll see ya'll when I get home. Make sure my sister is as happy as you seem to be."

"Cool. See you then."

CHAPTER SIXTEEN

WYATT

THE WEEKS after I told Kendra I loved her, have been life-altering. I didn't think there would be a time in my life that a woman would make me whole, and until Kendra, there wasn't. Now I can't picture my life without her in it. I am a changed man, and it was totally because of her.

Today we are having all of my friends over for dinner and she is so excited. I told her they are a bunch of assholes and normally they are, but with her they are different. Part of the reason is that they all know now that she's Malik's sister, but I think it's mostly because she has us all under some spell.

My girl is magical.

We get the steaks for dinner marinated and the pasta salad made before we sit down for a minute. It's nice to just relax on the couch, her legs resting across mine while I run my hand up and down them. The TV is on, but neither of us is paying attention. She is looking out the window and I am looking at her.

"Wyatt, how long ago did your dad pass away," she whispers turning her head to look at me.

"Almost three years ago. It was hard letting him go, but the cancer had taken over. As hard as it was for me, I know it was worse for him."

I hate talking about losing my dad. He was the only person I ever trusted, my only true friend besides Malik, but I feel like I have something like that with Kendra now. I know I can tell her anything without judgment.

"I'm so sorry. I remember him being a good and kind man. I wish Malik would have told me," she says, leaning over to kiss my arm.

"Me too, baby," I say and lean over, causing her to lie on her back as I climb onto of her. "He would have loved to see you again. I hope he knows that we've gotten together."

"He does." She reaches up running her hand down my face and smiles. "I love you."

I press my lips to hers then push my tongue into her mouth and we both moan from the contact. She wraps one leg around my hip, and I push my hips forward, letting her feel how much I want her. I reach my hand under her shirt and massage her tits, all the while never breaking our kiss.

"Damn, this is hot," I hear and pull away from Kendra, looking over my shoulder. There stands Todd, Joe, and Dave. "Don't stop on our account. I just didn't realize it was dinner and a show," Joe says.

I remove my hand from her tits as she unhooks her leg from me. Leaning down, I whisper in her ear, "To be continued." As I stand up, she sits up adjusting her shirt, and I shoot daggers at the three of them.

As pissed as I was when they interrupted us, now that we are sitting down to dinner and laughing at stories, I'm glad Kendra suggested this dinner. I can't remember a time that I hung out with the three of them that didn't include work, alcohol, or some random hook up. It's also great to see them accepting my new relationship with

Kendra. It's not that I needed their approval, Malik's is all I cared about, but it makes me happy that I have it.

"So this one time, Wyatt thinks he's going to show us how to pick up older chicks. He walks up to the sexiest woman in the bar and says some corny ass line and she throws her drink in his face," Todd says and they all laugh.

"At least I had the balls to talk to her. You guys were hiding behind a fucking door peeking through the crack." Kendra laughs even harder, and I wink at her.

"These are great stories. I think it's great you've all been friends for so long. I lost most of my friends when I went off to law school," she says before taking a sip of her wine.

"Why?" Todd asks finishing off his steak.

"I don't know. Probably because I spent more time studying than I did doing anything else." She looks over, silently begging me to change the subject.

"Hey guys, do you remember the time that Wayne got arrested because a visitor said he was trying to look into her cabin," I ask, and they all laugh.

Kendra mouths 'thank you' and I wink. Doesn't

she realize I would anything for her no matter how big or small?

After the guys finally leave and we clean dinner up, I toss her over my shoulder and carry her into my room then toss her on the bed.

"Hey!" she says, laughing.

I climb on top of her and tuck her hair behind her ears. "To be continued, remember?"

I press my lips to hers and she melts into me. Just like before, she wraps her leg around me and I massage her tits. This time I know no one is walking in. Laid out before me, she takes my breath away. I still can't believe that this stunning, sexy, smart woman loves me as much as I love her. I'm a lucky fucker.

She glances at my package, level with her eyes and reaches her hands up to lower my zipper. She runs her hand over the thickening bulge growing inside my jeans and her saucy eyes meet mine once more.

"Wyatt," she says on a moan.

She rises to her feet, slowly, and seductively as fuck. Just the smell of her makes my dick rock hard. All cherries and lace.

Our lips meet, and I make quick work with her shirt. It hits the floor. Her tits are better than I remember, and I should get an award with how much I picture them every night. She backs me up, pushing me down to sit on the couch. She moves between my legs.

"What color are your panties," I ask. My hand begins at the crook of her knee and travels up her smooth skin to the pleasure spot between her legs.

"Red."

I growl.

"And Lace," she finishes.

"Fuck, Kendra." She knows I love the red and lace together on her. The combination pops against her beautiful skin.

She unzips her shorts, letting them pool at her feet.

I run my hand higher up her silky leg as she steps out of them.

It's all white heat and red lace. Her body is an art of perfection, and her velvety skin screams for me to suck on her all day long.

Her fingers rummage through my hair as I reach both hands to cup her ass. I bring her to my lips, sucking the lace between my teeth.

She tastes good.

"Oh God," she breathes.

"Do you miss me? Does your pussy miss the way I make her feel?"

She nods as I suck along her sweet mound, sliding the panel of her panties aside with my finger. I lift her leg, planting her foot on the couch beside me so I can get a better taste.

She rocks her pussy against my face, digging her nails in my scalp and moaning all the while. My cock is hard and I want to lick her slit first.

It feels like it's been ages since I've dined on her sweet pussy. It's probably been more like two or three days. I lean back against the couch, lining her hot spot up with my hungry mouth.

I pull her panties to the side. I fuck her with my tongue as she grinds her clit against me. I slam a finger inside her as she loses control, rocking and fucking my face. I tug her ass closer, burying myself in her hot cunt. Fuck, she tastes amazing. I've missed her.

Note to self: eat my girl out every day.

CHAPTER SEVENTEEN

WYATT

KENDRA RIDES out the rest of her orgasm, screaming my name over and over. It's sexy as hell, and it makes me want to claim her once again.

"Wyatt!"

I lift her from the couch, carrying her back to the one bedroom in the back. I toss her on the bed and lower my jeans to the floor. Her sexy legs spread and I get a full view of her panty-covered pussy.

I climb the bed, mounting her as I run my hand down her neck. Her tits scream for me to touch them, cherish them.

I pay homage to her breasts, tugging and squeezing each pebbled peak. Lowering my mouth, I suck a nipple into my mouth and gently clamp down my teeth. She pulls my hair and I just bite harder. Sometimes my girl likes it rough, so that's how I give it to her.

She eggs me on with her moans and I flip her over and smack her ass, hard. Fuck, this girl drives me insane.

"Get that ass in the air." I yank at her hips, gripping her with all the want in me. "You know how I like it."

"Yes, baby."

Kissing down her neck to her tits I nip both her nipples poking through her bra, causing her to yell out.

"Yes!"

"Fuck, Kendra, I'll never get my fill of you."

She is so fucking sexy, I need to be inside of her. I rip off her panties and rub my hand down her pussy to see how wet she is. When her essence covers my fingers, I let out a groan. "So fucking wet."

My cock juts forth angrily as I remove my boxers and reach for the condom on my nightstand. She kisses my chest and lets her hands explore my body. Her soft touch makes it difficult to roll the condom on. "Your body is amazing, Wyatt. You are amazing."

I lay her back and kiss her lips. "No baby, you are."

She shakes her head and looks back at my chest. I lift her chin to look in my eyes and say, "I wish you could see yourself through my eyes. You'd see how breathtaking you are."

She smiles and runs her hand down my cheek. "I'm so lucky," she whispers.

"Baby, I'm the one who's lucky."

I kiss her and she runs her hands up and down my arm. I push my dick against her and she pushes back against me, letting me know she is just as ready as I am. I thrust into her causing her to scream out. I'm too turned on, too consumed with her. I need her to feel me everywhere, just like I feel her. Pumping myself in and out, fast and hard, I grunt every time she moans. It's hard and rough, yet somehow I feel like we are connecting more. Like she just took control of my entire heart, and damn it I hope I have hers.

She digs her nails into my arms and tosses her head back. "Oh God, Wyatt, I'm so close."

"Don't come until I tell you to."

"Wyatt, please."

"You feel so fucking good, baby," I growl out as I stroke deep inside of her.

"Wyatt, I need to come."

I can feel her tighten on my cock.

"Look at me, Kendra."

She does and I reach down to rub her clit.

"Come for me, baby. Now."

Seconds later, she explodes around me in orgasmic bliss. I look into her eyes watching her spiral. The look of pleasure on her face is so powerful that I can't hold back and my own orgasm rips through me. I keep my eyes focused on hers, hoping she too can see into my soul.

After we both recover, I get rid of the condom and pull her into my arms. "I love you so much, Kendra," I say, kissing her shoulder.

"I love you too, Wyatt," she replies, and I can hear the exhaustion in her voice.

"Sleep baby. I'll see you when I get off of work tomorrow."

She simply nods and I grin because even watching her fall asleep makes me happy.

～

LEAVING KENDRA IN MY BED, whether she's naked or not, is hard as hell. So when I get home after work, I can't wait to get to her place and pull her into my arms. I take a fast shower and throw on a pair of jeans and a blue t-shirt. I decide to take my truck and see if she wants to go grab something to eat. I pull up to her place and bounce up the stairs. I knock once and walk in.

I expect to see her waiting for me, maybe having a drink or hell sitting here in my old t-shirt. What I don't expect to see, what has my heart barely beating, is seeing her luggage in the living room. I spin around the cabin and notice that everything is packed up: the kitchen, the living room. I can even see out the back window that her patio table and chairs are put away.

What the fuck?

I'm so confused and starting to get nervous because maybe something is wrong.

"Kendra," I call out.

She walks out of the bedroom, pulling a suitcase behind her. She locks eyes with me and stops in her tracks.

"Wyatt," she whispers.

I try to step around all her crap to get to her

and when I do, she gives me a tight smile. "What the hell is going on? Are you going somewhere?"

"I got a call from my firm today and was offered this huge case," she says, looking at me with a smile cracking her lips.

"And you what? Weren't going to discuss it with me?"

"I have to work, Wyatt."

"Don't be so fucking condescending. You know what I mean."

I'm so pissed right now. I'm doing everything I can to control my temper.

"Baby, calm down."

I look at the bags of tied up trash by the door, the keys in her hand, and grow even angrier.

"So you just figured you'd pack up and hurry the hell out of here before I got off work? Were you even going to tell me you were leaving?"

"I wasn't just going to leave without saying goodbye."

"Looks like it."

"I wasn't."

"But you're leaving."

"Yes, but–"

"So that's it? You go back to New York and resume the boring fucking life you tried to escape?"

I know it sounds nasty, but she's the one who told me she wanted more. I was her fucking more.

"That's not fair. This case is huge, the firm expects me to step up, so I need to go. I'd regret it if I didn't," she says, pulling her suitcase to sit beside her. I shake my head and turn away from her.

"Wyatt, wait." I turn back around and she is smiling. "These last few weeks have been the best of my life and I do love you, but I need to do this. You can understand that right? This won't be forever."

I give my best fake smile and shake my head. "You said enough. Your only regret would be missing out on a huge case, not missing out on this," I say, pointing a finger between us.

She doesn't say anything so I turn toward the door. Pushing it open, I turn my head to look at her "This is why I don't do relationships. I told you, everyone always leaves."

With that, I let the screen door slam behind me and make my way to the truck. I've only felt this pain two other times, when my mom left and when my dad passed away.

Now I've lost Kendra, and I know that nothing will be the same again.

CHAPTER EIGHTEEN

KENDRA

IN THE MONTH I've been back in New York all I've done is work on this case. It's consumed me, and I think since my heart is bleeding, it's for the best. I haven't had time to think about how much I miss Wyatt.

Now I only dream about his voice, his touch, the way he made me feel, made me laugh. The beautiful places we picnicked, swimming at the lake, and hiking around the resort.

How did I get here? It all started with my brother. When Malik came into my cabin the morning I left, asking about Wyatt, things started to spiral out of control.

"Malik, you and daddy are home? Mom said you guys would be gone for six weeks."

"I thought I needed to come home early."

"Why?"

"Were you with Wyatt last night?"

"Yes...but what's wrong? Wyatt said that you gave us your blessing."

"I did, baby girl, but I had a chance to think about it and while Wyatt is a good man, I don't think he's the man for you."

"Why?!"

"What are you going to do, Kendra? Move here and practice law in the village? Or is he going to landscape and work on cabins in Manhattan? You see where I'm going with this? The two of you can never work out in real life because one of you will have to sacrifice too much."

"No one is sacrificing anything, we're just living in the moment right now."

"That's nice, but living in the moment can get people hurt. Two people I love. It won't work, baby girl. Leave him alone. It's not worth the damage it could cause to all three of us."

But I wasn't giving up. I made my brother some chocolate chip pancakes and then we debated for a little longer that morning. I told him I'd fallen in love, but then he told me flat out that Wyatt was not capable of returning my feelings. That Wyatt was fooling himself. And that if I wanted to protect myself, my heart, I'd leave.

I still didn't believe him.

We fought long that morning. Damn did we fight. And when it comes to me, I discovered that my brother fights dirty.

The more stories I heard about the old Wyatt, the more I started to wonder if our relationship was just something I wanted so badly, that I didn't see the truth. That perhaps I had convinced myself of this amazing relationship that wasn't real.

That's when fear set in, reality came crashing down, and when I got the call later that morning for this law case...I ran.

"Kendra, it's going to be another all-nighter, so you better order some food for yourself," my boss says to me as he gets ready to leave for the night.

"Okay," I say as he closes my door. Another all-nighter by myself.

After eating Chinese takeout and working

several hours, I drop my pen and rub my eyes. Exhaustion is setting in, yet I have so much more to do. I type on the computer and as the words blur together, I shake my head. I need to get a little sleep. Thankfully, I have a small couch in my office and I climb onto it letting sleep pull me under.

I see empty, hollowed, eyes. Those haunting eyes, so sad and hurt. I'm standing in my cabin back at Day's Ranch, and I feel those eyes on me no matter where I go. To avoid them, I decide to go sit outside, hiding from their hard gaze.

I smile when I breathe in the air. It smells crisp and fresh, like wildflowers and the woods. It's intoxicating, making me happy I came back. Looking over to the right I see muddy footprints, and I cock my head because I don't remember seeing them when I walked out here. My curiosity gets the best of me and I get up to see where they lead.

I follow them all the way to the lake and they seem to just disappear, but out of the corner of my eye, I see more. The day has suddenly turned to night and a cool breeze has me rubbing my hands on my arms, but I still need to find out where these footprints are leading.

I blink my eyes and I'm inside a grotto. It looks

so familiar, yet I can't place it. Have I been here before or maybe just dreamt about it? The moonlight shining in is beautiful and lets me see just how stunning it is in here.

When I hear footsteps, I know it is whoever I am looking for. Part of me is excited, but part of me is nervous. I sit down on a log and wait as the footsteps grow nearer. I hear leaves moving and bite my lip waiting to see who exactly it was that has lured me here to this little piece of paradise.

"You're the only person I've ever brought here. It took years to make and I'm so glad you like it," I hear a familiar voice say and jump up.

"Wow. I'm the only girl you've ever brought here?" a high pitched, squeaky voice says.

"Yes, you are. Now let's have sex because you are beautiful and I love you," he says, and I suddenly can see the two people.

One of them is Wyatt and the other, I have no idea who she is, but she is loving the attention he is paying her. He's lying to her because I'm the only one he's brought here. I remember now. This is Wyatt's grotto, and this is where we had our first unofficial date.

Just as I smile thinking of the memories he kisses her, and I start to cry. "Wyatt, no! Wyatt, stop, please! I'm here, Wyatt, I'm here," I scream trying to get his attention, but it's no use. He doesn't hear me, doesn't see me, yet I hear and see it all.

How could he do this, just forget me so quickly and bring someone else here? I'm sobbing trying to get him to notice me, and when I realize he never will...

I wake up screaming.

Holy shit, it was just a dream. I hold my hand over my pounding heart and take a second to gather my thoughts. That's when I realize I'm actually crying, heavy tears running down my face. "It was only a dream, yet it felt so real," I whisper to myself as I stand up to get a sip of water.

After calming myself down, I shake the thoughts of my dream and get back to work. The only sound I hear is the clicking of my keyboard. I look over toward the clock and say, "The damn clock."

Wyatt was right. I just ran back to the same boring life I had. The same life I've always had. Why the fuck did I do that? Malik had no right to interfere, but ultimately it was me who decided to leave. Ultimately, it was me who ran like a frightened animal.

I was so happy there, so in love. What have I done?

I jump up and grab my things before writing a quick note to my boss. Good thing I got a few hours of sleep, because I intend to drive until I reach...home.

CHAPTER NINETEEN

KENDRA

IT TAKES close to three hours of straight driving, but I finally pull up to my cabin. I called my mom on the way there and she told me it was still unoccupied and that I could stay there if I wanted. She'd leave the key under the creepy gargoyle figurine guarding it.

The second I see my place my heart beats faster. I hate that the last memory I have of it is the sadness on Wyatt's face. I shake my head and grab my suitcase before going inside. I take a deep breath and smile. "I'm home."

After sleeping until dusk, I get up and take a

shower making sure to do my hair and makeup to perfection. My nerves are getting the best of me, but I need to find Wyatt. I have a lot to apologize for, and I can only hope that he will take me back.

I step outside into the cool air and wrap my arms around myself. Without even thinking, I head straight for the grotto. I don't know why, maybe it was my dream or maybe it was that this is where I starting to fall for him.

Either way, my feet carry me and before I know it I'm ducking under the branches. As soon as I step in the air in my lungs is sucked out. It's empty, yet I feel Wyatt all around me. I walk over to a log and sit down.

Looking around makes my heart hurt. I've really fucked up. I never should have left, I should have followed my heart. He will never forgive me. I did the one thing he's always feared. I left him.

I sit for a while and when I realize this isn't getting me anywhere; I stand up. Just as I walk toward the only way out, I hear leaves rustling in the wind and my pulse picks up. What if Wyatt is actually bringing a woman in here. As much as it hurts to think that, how could I blame him? I did exactly what he feared, I left him, and it's been a month of zero contact.

I stand frozen in place and the second Wyatt steps into view my knees go weak. In that moment, seeing him after a month, I know that he is my world.

"Kendra? What the hell are you doing here," he asks with a bite in his tone that I expect.

"Looking for you," I say, hoping he will hear me out.

He crosses his arms over his chest and keeps his distance from me. Even if he doesn't accept my apology, I still need to do it. He deserves that at the very least.

"Remember when we first met, and you were so pissed because I didn't believe you when you said nothing happened with us?" He gives a slight nod of his head and I'm grateful to have his attention, it spurs me on.

"Remember how you went out of your way to make sure I knew what happened, that I knew what an amazing guy you really are?" I move a bit closer to him and he doesn't budge an inch. "That's what I'm doing now. I need you to know how sorry I am.

I was selfish and hurtful. You were right; I ran back to New York to continue with my boring life the second I got scared. The thing is, I finally realized the reason my life is boring, unfulfilled, and lonely in New York is because that isn't where I belong. I belong here, with you."

I move to stand right in front of him and I want to reach out and touch him, but he still has a hard look on his face. "It took you leaving to realize that? I fucking knew that long before you left," he says looking through me.

"I fucked up," I whisper. "I made a mistake. Can you forgive me?"

"You left, Kendra, just like I knew you would. I don't know why you want to come back just to leave again," he says with more hurt in his voice this time.

"I left here; but I didn't leave you, not completely." I take a chance and rest my hand on his arm, and I feel the muscle flex beneath the skin. "I left my heart with you."

"You didn't even call me."

"You didn't call me."

"I wasn't the one who walked out."

"But I missed you just the same if not more."

He searches my eyes looking for the truth and I let him because I have nothing to hide. With my pulse racing and my heart in his hands, I take a leap. A leap to my happiness, my future, my forever.

"I'm so sorry I hurt you. I can't say it enough, but I'd like to make it up to you for the rest of our lives."

I can't help the tears that run down my cheeks, but I continue, "I love you, Wyatt, and I want to come back. Can you give me another chance? A chance to prove it to you, like you proved it to me?"

I don't know what else to say, yet I feel I need to say so much more.

In an instant he pulls me into his arms and my tears are unstoppable. He holds me so tight to him that it's hard to breathe, but I don't give a shit.

"Kendra, this last month has been as hard if not harder than losing my parents. I don't know if I can trust you completely or even if I forgive you, but fuck I need you," he says, and I hear the emotion in his voice. "I missed you."

He releases his hold on me slightly and presses his lips to mine. I don't know what the future holds, but I know for sure it includes Wyatt, because I didn't know what living was, until him.

"I'll earn your forgiveness, baby." I tell him. "Even it takes a lifetime."

EPILOGUE

One Year Later
WYATT

THE LAST SIX months have been the best of my life. Kendra moved home to Day's Ranch and even though it took time to fix all the wounds, we worked through it all. It wasn't easy, and it took a great deal of trust and honesty, but damn it's been worth it.

She's even helped me overcome some of the trauma I faced from my time in the war. She has been there with me through it all. I love her more than I ever thought I was capable of. More than I've ever loved anyone. I am a lucky son of a bitch. After all the women I've casually slept with, I've found my happily ever after. Not every man can say that shit.

After we worked through everything and I mean everything, Malik proved to be our most difficult obstacle. I should have known our conversation went to easily. Malik needs to process shit. He can't be put on the spot, which is what I did when I called him while he was on his hunting trip.

I think though when he saw me after Kendra left; he started to realize that feelings were real. When she came back, we talked with her parents and Malik, making sure they knew I was in this as much, if not more, than she was. I needed to make sure they all understood that I would never stifle Kendra's ambition or her dreams. I just want her to make new ones here with me. And she is.

When she told me she quit her job in New York, it was the beginning of her getting my trust back. I knew she was in this one hundred percent. She talked to her mom, who helped Kendra get a job with Jason Dickson; the lawyer who runs a small law firm in town. She didn't want to give up law and now that she is working with Jason, she doesn't need to. Once he retires, he's handing her the practice on a silver platter.

Then we decided to move in together. Malik got sick of watching us creeping out of each other's cabin's every morning and I agreed. Neither of us wanted to live off the property or eliminate cabin living, this place holds too many memories, so we ended up buying a larger cabin near the grotto that I have been restoring for the last year. It is beautiful, huge, and the perfect home to share with the woman I love.

"Wyatt?" I turn to the sound of Kendra's sweet voice. "Are you sure we got enough food? I mean there's a lot of people coming today."

I chuckle and pull her into my arms. "Baby, relax. They are coming to celebrate our engagement. They should be bringing us food." She smacks my chest and I laugh. "We have plenty of food, plenty of drinks, and plenty of time."

She pulls back a bit and searches my face. "Plenty of time?"

I lean down, nipping her ear and whisper, "For me to worship your body."

She shivers and emits a soft moan. I check my watch and pull her into our bedroom for a quickie before our guests arrive today. I need to touch her. I always want to touch this woman.

She lies on the bed, her russet skin highlighted by the sun streaming through the windows. She's so fucking perfect it's insane to me how I could have ever been so lucky.

My fingers brush along the base of her scalp, into the tresses of her thick hair. It never surprises me how she always turns me on with just a whisper of my name on her lips.

"Wyatt," she breathes.

My dick grows incredibly hard, harder than the last time I was inside her, straining against the zipper of my jeans. And she knows with a smile as she pulls me out. I climb out of my shorts and boxers and lift the hem of her dress.

"Fuck, I want you so bad."

She knows I do. She always knows how badly I want her.

"I want you too but the time–"

Fuck the time. I move her to the bed, and run my fingers up her long legs, discarding her dress on the way up. She's even more stunning in her black panties and bra.

She knows I'm going to fuck her. There's no

discussing it. The guests are just going to have to wait.

I lie her down on the bed and get ready to take her. To claim her. To let her know who's in charge. To let her know how much I love her.

I remove her panties with my teeth and suck along her skin as soon as they're out of the way. She moans long and hard for me, her fingers digging into my scalp. But it doesn't last, because there's only one thing I want to do to this woman, get deep inside her and make her come all over me. I quickly flip her over on her stomach.

"Hands and knees, Kendra."

She quickly obeys and once in position, I waste no time pushing at her entrance as she moans with sweet agony. I spread her knees a bit farther as I enter her in one punishing thrust. Fuck she feels so good.

Better than last time. I swear she keeps getting better and better. Like a fine wine.

I mutter something nonsensical as I stroke inside of her. It feels exquisite. Like a tight vise squeezing the life out of my dick.

And this woman is all mine. She's given every part of herself to me. And I cherish it all. Reveling in the fact this woman loves me back.

Her sharp red nails claw at our poor goose down pillows for life as I pump inside her, going deeper with each thrust.

My hands are all over her now. I reach under and squeeze her nipples. I slap her ass a couple of times. Then I slide my palm into her lustrous locks and pull. Making sure to ride her pussy until she begs for release.

She's my own personal sanctuary and her moans increase as I keep fucking her. My girl likes it rough and lately has been wanting it harder and harder each time. So, I don't hold back. I fuck her as hard as I can. And she loves it. She's hungry for it.

I'm starving as well and this is all I want to eat.

I can't even think about how soon our house will be filled with guests, my only thought is on making her come. On taking this woman to the point of no return. So I keep pumping inside her. Keep pushing and screwing her until I can barely hang on.

"Better be quiet, baby. The guests are coming."

She moans so loudly I swear the whole neighborhood can hear her, and I kind of hope they do. Her fucking moans drive me crazy with a lust so deep it's hard to contain. She moans louder, and I nip at her shoulder, the smooth skin beneath my teeth. I love tasting her. She tastes so good.

"Don't come yet," I order with a feral grunt.

I pump harder as one hand reaches down to play with the bundle of nerves between her legs. I push and pull and before I know it she's screaming out her release like a good little girl.

"Fuck!" she screams. "Wyatt, I'm coming."

I keep fucking her, wanting more than anything to get her off one more time before our guests arrive.

And she knows I won't stop until she is coming all over me again. Her pussy feels so good, so tight with her release helping my dick glide in faster and rougher.

She twists her neck around, and her eyes crash into mine, making me forget about everything but being here with her. She's my safe place.

"I love you," I tell her as I continue to move deep inside her.

Her head falls back down. "I love you too."

And I believe her.

I always believe her, because she shows me daily how much she loves me.

We have a good thing here, one I won't ever

take for granted. She's everything to me. And I won't ever let her forget how much I love her.

"Wyatt," she says almost breathlessly. "I can't."

"Yes, baby, you can."

I slap one of her ass cheeks, which seems to be the little push she needed, and she comes again, and I find my orgasm right after her. Wanting nothing more than to be together forever. We calm our breathing and fix ourselves all before the first guests arrive.

If you would have asked me two years ago if I thought I'd get married, I would have said no way. But that all changed the second my eyes landed on Kendra. She's made me a better person, a man that I'm proud to be. Who enjoys life, trusts with all his heart, and loves furiously. Kendra is the reason I discovered the man I was supposed to be, because my life was incomplete until her.

The real me was wounded from childhood, from war, and I spent an enormous amount of time just trying to hide from it all. Just trying to pretend I was braver than I was.

I used women. I didn't care about anyone because I was afraid of myself. I was afraid of losing someone like I lost my mother. I lost brothers in the war. Men I cared about more than anything.

And I was so afraid to open my heart up and ever let anyone else in. But, Kendra opened me up to the possibility that life can be better. That things will be okay. That my life was meant for more if I just gave myself permission.

I want to be the man she deserves. She's a strong woman, who deserves an equally strong man to stand by her side. I love her and always will. Together we can overcome anything. Together we can do anything we want. Together we are powerful.

Apart we are a mess.

Note to self: never be apart from Kendra again.

EXTENDED EPILOGUE

KENDRA

THE BEST THINGS in life come to those who aren't looking for it. I wasn't looking to fall in love with Wyatt, but I did. I feel so in love, I can barely breathe sometimes.

He's the kindest man on the planet and takes care of me when I need it. My parents raised me to be fiercely independent, but sometimes it feels good to let go, and let someone take care of me from time to time.

I think that's the beauty of love. Our love. You find your strength in others, but you also find your weaknesses there too. And together you become a whole unit, strong, and never breakable.

I love Wyatt, and it was hard at first. With my parents a little unsure. My brother a lot unsure. It was difficult to always trust that I'd made the right decision. But after a while, they've all come to see the man I see when I look into his eyes.

A good man.

An honest man.

The perfect man for me.

Every touch, every kiss, it all rings true for me. And I love him more and more every day.

We are getting married tomorrow, and I am nervous as can be. Not because I'm afraid he might not be the one. I know he is. But I guess because I'm afraid I might not live up to who he thinks I am. Who he deserves.

He honors me both spiritually and physically in a way that I never thought was possible. Can a man truly love and respect a woman like he does me and there's no catch? I don't know. I guess I'll find out because I am marrying this man tomorrow come hell or high water.

Married.

Can you believe it? I never thought I'd be marrying my brother's best friend.

Who's now my best friend.

The sexy soldier who stole my heart.

The man I love more than anyone else in the world.

I'm so glad I listened to my inner voice telling me to come back home. My destiny was waiting for me here. My destiny fulfilled begins tomorrow.

I am so happy.

We're going to have an amazing life together in our cabin, under the stars.

"You ready, Kendra?" my brother Malik calls out as he knocks at the door.

"Come in."

"You look amazing little sis'"

"Thank you." I smile.

"You still want to do this right?"

I giggle. "I definitely do."

I put on another coat of red lip gloss on my lips. Wyatt's favorite color.

"Wait until you see the truck. Mom and dad decorated it special for you. It's all girly and shit."

Malik kisses me on the cheek.

"You ready to get married to your man at the grotto today?"

"Yep...I'm so ready."

"Then let's go and get your next chapter started."

～

THANK YOU FOR READING WYATT. It is the first novel in the Overwatch Division Series, and I hope you enjoyed it. **Next up is my next military romance, ASA. Grab it at its lowest price or for free on Kindle Unlimited today.**

～

PLEASE SIGN Up To Be Notified when my next release is live and don't forget to leave a review if you've enjoyed this novel. I appreciate the encouraging words more than you know.

You can also chat with me on Facebook.

Or follow me on Instagram.

ALSO BY COCO MILLER

Big City Billionaires

Faking For Mr. Pope

Virgin Escort For Mr. Vaughn

Pretending for Mr. Parker

Red Bratva Billionaires

MAXIM

SERGEI

VIKTOR

The Overwatch Division

WYATT

ASA

CESAR